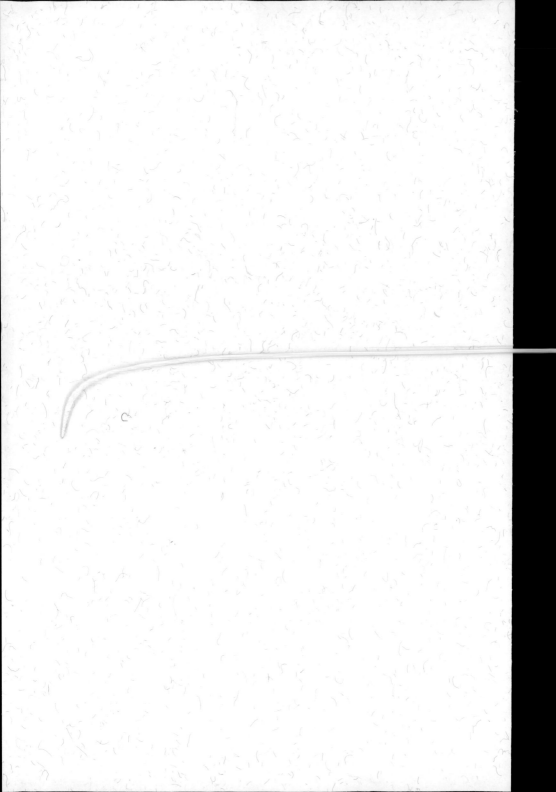

THE
LOVED ONE

OTHER WORKS BY EVELYN WAUGH

NOVELS

Decline and Fall

Vile Bodies

Black Mischief

A Handful of Dust

Scoop

Put Out More Flags

Work Suspended

Brideshead Revisited

Scott King's Modern Europe

Helena

Men at Arms

Love Among the Ruins

Officers and Gentlemen

The End of the Battle

The Ordeal of Gilbert Pinfold

STORIES

*Mr. Loveday's Little Outing,
and Other Sad Stories*

Tactical Exercise

Basil Seal Rides Again

Charles Ryder's Schooldays

*The Complete Stories
of Evelyn Waugh*

BIOGRAPHY

Rossetti

Edmund Campion

Msgr. Ronald Knox

AUTOBIOGRAPHY/DIARIES/LETTERS

A Little Learning

The Diaries of Evelyn Waugh

The Letters of Evelyn Waugh

TRAVEL/JOURNALISM

A Bachelor Abroad

They Were Still Dancing

Ninety-Two Days

Waugh in Abyssinia

Mexico: An Object Lesson

When the Going Was Good

A Tourist in Africa

A Little Order

*The Essays, Articles and Reviews
of Evelyn Waugh*

EVELYN WAUGH

THE LOVED ONE

An Anglo-American Tragedy

BARNES & NOBLE *Modern Classics*

To
Nancy Mitford

A Warning

This is a purely fanciful tale, a little nightmare produced by the unaccustomed high living of a brief visit to Hollywood. Readers whose pleasure in fiction derives from identifying the characters and scenes with real people and real places will be disappointed. If in the vast variety of life in America there is anyone at all like any of the characters I have invented, I can only remind that person that we never met, and assure him or her that, had we done so, I would not have attempted to portray a living individual in a book where all the incidents are entirely imaginary.

As I have said, this is a nightmare and in parts, perhaps, somewhat gruesome. The squeamish should return their copies to the library or the bookstore unread.

ONE

——— ❧⋯❧ ———

A
LL DAY THE HEAT HAD BEEN BARELY SUPPORTABLE
but at evening a breeze arose in the West, blowing
from the heart of the setting sun and from the
ocean, which lay unseen, unheard behind the scrubby
foothills. It shook the rusty fringes of palm-leaf and swelled
the dry sounds of summer, the frog-voices, the grating ci-
cadas, and the ever present pulse of music from the neigh-
bouring native huts.

In that kindly light the stained and blistered paint of the
bungalow and the plot of weeds between the veranda and the
dry water-hole lost their extreme shabbiness, and the two
Englishmen, each in his rocking-chair, each with his whisky
and soda and his out-dated magazine, the counterparts of
numberless fellow-countrymen exiled in the barbarous re-
gions of the world, shared in the brief illusory rehabilitation.

"Ambrose Abercrombie will be here shortly," said the
elder. "I don't know why. He left a message he would come.
Find another glass, Dennis, if you can." Then he added
more petulantly: "Kierkegaard, Kafka, Connolly, Compton
Burnet, Sartre, 'Scottie' Wilson. Who are they? What do
they want?"

"I've heard of some of them. They were being talked
about in London at the time I left."

"They talked of 'Scottie' Wilson?"

"No. I don't think so. Not of him."

"That's 'Scottie' Wilson. Those drawings there. Do they make any sense to you?"

"No."

"No."

Sir Francis Hinsley's momentary animation subsided. He let fall his copy of *Horizon* and gazed towards the patch of deepening shadow which had once been a pool. His was a weak, sensitive, intelligent face, blurred somewhat by soft living and long boredom. "It was Hopkins once," he said; "Joyce and Freud and Gertrude Stein. I couldn't make any sense of *them* either. I never was much good at anything new. 'Arnold Bennett's debt to Zola'; 'Flecker's debt to Henley.' That was the nearest I went to the moderns. My best subjects were 'The English Parson in English Prose' or 'Cavalry Actions with the Poets'—that kind of thing. People seemed to like them once. Then they lost interest. I did too. I was always the most defatigable of hacks. I needed a change. I've never regretted coming away. The climate suits me. They are a very decent, generous lot of people out here and *they don't expect you to listen.* Always remember that, dear boy. It's the secret of social ease in this country. They talk entirely for their own pleasure. Nothing they say is designed to be heard."

"Here comes Ambrose Abercrombie," said the young man.

"Evening, Frank. Evening, Barlow," said Sir Ambrose Abercrombie coming up the steps. "It's been another scorcher, eh? Mind if I take a pew? When," he added aside to the young man who helped him to whisky. "Right up with soda, please."

Sir Ambrose wore dark grey flannels, an Eton Rambler tie, an I Zingari ribbon in his boater hat. This was his invariable dress on sunny days; whenever the weather allowed it he wore a deer-stalker cap and an Inverness cape. He was still on what Lady Abercrombie fatuously called the "right" side of sixty but after many years of painfully attempting to look youthful, he now aspired to the honours of age. It was his latest quite vain wish that people should say of him: "Grand old boy."

"Been meaning to look you up for a long time. Trouble about a place like this one's so darn busy, one gets in a groove and loses touch. Doesn't do to lose touch. We limeys have to stick together. You shouldn't hide yourself away, Frank, you old hermit."

"I remember a time when you lived not so far away."

"Did I? 'Pon my soul I believe you're right. That takes one back a bit. It was before we went to Beverly Hills. Now, as of course you know, we're in Bel Air. But to tell you the truth I'm getting a bit restless there. I've got a bit of land out on Pacific Palisades. Just waiting for building costs to drop. Where was it I used to live? Just across the street, wasn't it?"

Just across the street, twenty years or more ago, when this neglected district was the centre of fashion, Sir Francis, in prime middle-age, was then the only knight in Hollywood, the doyen of English society, chief script-writer in Megalopolitan Pictures and President of the Cricket Club. Then the young, or youngish, Ambrose Abercrombie used to bounce about the lots in his famous series of fatiguing roles, acrobatic heroic historic, and come almost nightly to Sir Francis for refreshment. English titles abounded now in Hollywood, several of them authentic, and Sir Ambrose had been known to speak slightingly of Sir Francis as a "Lloyd George creation." The seven league boots of failure had carried the old and the ageing man far apart. Sir Francis had descended to the Publicity Department and now held rank, one of a dozen, as Vice-President of the Cricket Club. His swimming pool which had once flashed like an aquarium with the limbs of long-departed beauties was empty now and cracked and over-grown with weed.

Yet there was a chivalric bond between the two.

"How are things at Megalo?" asked Sir Ambrose.

"Greatly disturbed. We are having trouble with Juanita del Pablo."

" 'Luscious, languid and lustful'?"

"Those are not the correct epithets. She is—or rather was—'surly, lustrous and sadistic.' I should know because I composed the phrase myself. It was a 'smash-hit,' as they say, and set a new note in personal publicity.

"Miss del Pablo has been a particular protégée of mine from the first. I remember the day she arrived. Poor Leo bought her for her eyes. She was called Baby Aaronson then—splendid eyes and a fine head of black hair. So Leo made her Spanish. He had most of her nose cut off and sent her to Mexico for six weeks to learn flamenco singing. Then he handed her over to me. *I* named her. *I* made her an anti-Fascist refugee. *I* said she hated men because of her treatment by Franco's Moors. That was a new angle then. It caught on. And she was really quite good in her way, you know—with a truly horrifying natural scowl. Her legs were never *photogénique* but we kept her in long skirts and used an understudy for the lower half in scenes of violence. I was proud of her and she was good for another ten years' work at least.

"And now there's been a change of policy at the top. We are only making healthy films this year to please the Catholic League of Decency. So poor Juanita has to start at the beginning again as an Irish colleen. They've bleached her hair and dyed it vermilion. I told them colleens were dark but the technicolor men insisted. She's working ten hours a day learning the brogue and to make it harder for the poor girl they've pulled all her teeth out. She never had to smile before and her own set was good enough for a snarl. Now she'll have to laugh roguishly all the time. That means dentures.

"I've spent three days trying to find a name to please her. She's turned everything down. Maureen—there are two here already; Deirdre—no one could pronounce it; Oonagh—sounds Chinese; Bridget—too common. The truth is she's in a thoroughly nasty temper."

Sir Ambrose, in accordance with local custom, had refrained from listening.

"Ah," he said, "healthy films. All for 'em. I said to the Knife and Fork Club, 'I've always had two principles throughout all my life in motion-pictures: never do before the camera what you would not do at home and never do at home what you would not do before the camera.' "

He enlarged this theme while Sir Francis, in his turn, sequestered his thoughts. Thus the two knights sat for nearly an hour, side by side in their rocking-chairs, alternately eloquent and abstracted, gazing into the gloaming through their monocles while the young man from time to time refilled their glasses and his own.

The time was apt for reminiscence and in his silent periods Sir Francis strayed back a quarter of a century and more to foggy London streets lately set free for all eternity from fear of the Zeppelin; to Harold Monro reading aloud at the Poetry Bookshop; Blunden's latest in the *London Mercury*; Robin de la Condamine at the Phoenix matinees; luncheon with Maud in Grosvenor Square, tea with Gosse in Hanover Terrace; eleven neurotic ballad-mongers in a Fleet Street pub just off for a day's cricket in Metroland, the boy with the galley-proofs plucking at his sleeve; numberless toasts at numberless banquets to numberless Immortal Memories . . .

Sir Ambrose had a more adventurous past but he lived existentially. He thought of himself as he was at that moment, brooded fondly on each several excellence and rejoiced.

"Well," he said at length, "I should be toddling. Mustn't keep the missus waiting"; but he made no move and turned instead to the young man. "And how are things with you, Barlow? We haven't seen you on the cricket field lately. Very busy at Megalo, I suppose?"

"No. As a matter of fact my contract ran out three weeks ago."

"I say, did it? Well, I expect you're glad of a rest. I know I should be." The young man did not answer. "If you'll take my advice, just sit easy for a time until something attractive turns up. Don't jump at the first thing. These fellows out here respect a man who knows his own value. Most important to keep the respect of these fellows.

"We limeys have a peculiar position to keep up, you know, Barlow. They may laugh at us a bit—the way we talk and the way we dress; our monocles—they may think us cliquey and stand-offish, but, by God, they respect us. Your five-to-two is a judge of quality. He knows what he's buying and it's only the finest type of Englishman that you meet out here. I often feel like an ambassador, Barlow. It's a responsibility, I can tell you, and in various degrees every Englishman out here shares it. We can't all be at the top of the tree but we are all men of responsibility. You never find an Englishman among the under-dogs—except in England, of course. That's understood out here, thanks to the example we've set. There are jobs that an Englishman just doesn't take.

"We had an unfortunate case some years ago of a very decent young fellow who came out as a scene designer. Clever chap but he went completely native—wore ready-made shoes, and a belt instead of braces, went about without a tie, ate at drug-stores. Then, if you'll believe it, he left the studio and opened a restaurant with an Italian partner. Got cheated, of course, and the next thing he was behind a bar shaking cocktails. Appalling business. We raised a subscription at the Cricket Club to send him home, but the blighter wouldn't go. Said he liked the place, if you please. That man did irreparable harm, Barlow. He was nothing less than a deserter. Luckily the war came. He went home then all right and got himself

killed in Norway. He atoned, but I always think how much
better not to have anything to atone for, eh?

"Now you're a man of reputation in your own line, Barlow. If you weren't you wouldn't be here. I don't say poets
are much in demand but they're bound to want one again
sooner or later and when they do, they'll come to you cap in
hand—if you haven't done anything in the meantime to lose
their respect. See what I mean?

"Well, here I am talking like a Dutch uncle while the missus is waiting for her dinner. I must toddle. So long, Frank,
I've enjoyed our talk. Wish we saw you more often at the
Cricket Club. Good-bye, young man, and just remember
what I've been saying. I may look like an old buffer but I
know what I'm talking about. Don't move, either of you. I
can find my way."

It was quite dark now. The head-lamps of the waiting car
spread a brilliant fan of light behind the palm trees, swept
across the front of the bungalow and receded towards Hollywood Boulevard.

"What do you make of that?" said Dennis Barlow.

"He's heard something. That was what brought him here."

"It was bound to come out."

"Certainly. If exclusion from British society can be
counted as martyrdom, prepare for the palm and the halo.
You have not been to your place of business today?"

"I'm on the night shift. I actually managed to write today.
Thirty lines. Would you like to see them?"

"No," said Sir Francis. "It is one of the numberless com-
pensations of my exile that I need never read unpublished

verses—or, for that matter, verses in any condition. Take
them away, dear boy, prune and polish at your leisure. They
would only distress me. I should not understand them and I
might be led to question the value of a sacrifice which I now
applaud. You are a young man of genius, the hope of English poetry. I have heard it said and I devoutly believe it. I
have served the cause of art enough by conniving at your
escape from a bondage to which I myself have been long
happily reconciled.

"Did they ever, when you were a child, take you to a
Christmas play called *Where the Rainbow Ends*—a very silly
piece? Saint George and a midshipman flew off on a carpet to
rescue some lost children from a Dragon's country. It always
seemed to me a gross interference. The children were perfectly happy. They paid tribute, I remember, of their letters
from home, unopened. Your verses are my letters from
home—like Kierkegaard and Kafka and 'Scottie' Wilson. I
pay without protest or resentment. Fill my glass, dear boy. I
am your *memento mori*. I am deep in thrall to the Dragon
King. Hollywood is my life.

"Did you see the photograph some time ago in one of
the magazines of a dog's head severed from its body,
which the Russians are keeping alive for some obscene
Muscovite purpose by pumping blood into it from a bottle? It dribbles at the tongue when it smells a cat. That's
what all of us are, you know, out here. The studios keep us
going with a pump. We are still just capable of a few crude
reactions—nothing more. If we ever got disconnected
from our bottle, we should simply crumble. I like to think

that it was the example of myself before your eyes day after day for more than a year that inspired your heroic resolution to set up in an independent trade. You have had example and perhaps now and then precept. I may have counselled you in so many words to leave the studio while you could still do so."

"You did. A thousand times."

"Surely not so often? Once or twice when I was in liquor. Not a thousand times. And my advice, I think, was to return to Europe. I never suggested anything so violently macabre, so Elizabethan, as the work you chose. Tell me, do you give your new employer satisfaction, do you think?"

"My manner is congenial. He told me so yesterday. The man they had before caused offence by his gusto. They find me reverent. It is my combination of melancholy with the English accent. Several of our clientele have commented favourably upon it."

"But our fellow expatriates? We cannot expect sympathy from them. What did our late visitor say? 'There are jobs that an Englishman just doesn't take.' Yours, dear boy, is pre-eminently one of those."

Dennis Barlow went to work after dinner. He drove towards Burbank, past luminous motels, past the golden gates and flood-lit temples of Whispering Glades Memorial Park, almost to the extremity of the city, to his place of business. His colleague, Miss Myra Poski, was waiting for relief, hatted and freshly painted.

"I hope I'm not late."

"You're sweet. I've a date at the Planetarium or I'd stay and fix you some coffee. There's been nothing to do all day except mail a few remembrance cards. Oh, and Mr. Schultz says if anything comes in put it straight on the ice this hot weather. Good-bye"; and she was gone leaving Dennis in sole charge of the business.

The office was furnished in sombre good taste that was relieved by a pair of bronze puppies on the chimney-piece. A low trolley of steel and white enamel alone distinguished the place from a hundred thousand modern American reception-rooms; that and the clinical smell. A bowl of roses stood beside the telephone; their scent contended with the carbolic, but did not prevail.

Dennis sat in one of the arm-chairs, put his feet on the trolley and settled himself to read. Life in the Air Force had converted him from an amateur to a mere addict. There were certain trite passages of poetry which from a diverse multitude of associations never failed to yield the sensations he craved; he never experimented; these were the branded drug, the sure specific, big magic. He opened the anthology as a woman opens her familiar pack of cigarettes.

Outside the windows the cars swept past continuously, out of town, into town, lights ablaze, radios at full throttle.

"I wither slowly in thine arms," he read. *"Here at the quiet limit of the world,"* and repeated to himself: "Here at the quiet limit of the world. Here at the quiet limit of the world" . . . as a monk will repeat a single pregnant text, over and over again in prayer.

Presently the telephone rang.

"The Happier Hunting Ground," he said.

A woman's voice came to him, hoarse, it seemed, with
emotion; in other circumstances he might have thought
her drunk. "This is Theodora Heinkel, Mrs. Walter
Heinkel, of 207 Via Dolorosa, Bel Air. You must come at
once. I can't tell you over the phone. My little Arthur—
they've just brought him in. He went out first thing and
never came back. I didn't worry because he's sometimes
been away like that before. I said to Mr. Heinkel, 'But,
Walter, I can't go out to dine when I don't know where
Arthur is' and Mr. Heinkel said, 'What the heck? You can't
walk out on Mrs. Leicester Scrunch at the last minute,' so
I went and there I was at the table on Mr. Leicester
Scrunch's right hand when they brought me the news . . .
Hullo, hullo, are you there?"

Dennis picked up the instrument which he had laid on the
blotting pad. "I will come at once, Mrs. Heinkel; 207 Via Dolorosa I think you said."

"I said I was sitting at Mr. Leicester Scrunch's right hand
when they brought me the news. He and Mr. Heinkel had to
help me to the automobile."

"I am coming at once."

"I shall never forgive myself as long as I live. To think of
his being brought home alone. The maid was out and the city
wagon-driver had to telephone from the drug-store . . .
Hullo, hullo. Are you there? I said the city wagon-driver had
to telephone from the drug-store."

"I am on my way, Mrs. Heinkel."

Dennis locked the office and backed the car from the

garage; not his own, but the plain black van which was used for official business. Half an hour later he was at the house of mourning. A corpulent man came down the garden path to greet him. He was formally dressed for the evening in the high fashion of the place—Donegal tweeds, sandals, a grass-green silk shirt, open at the neck with an embroidered monogram covering half his torso. "Am I pleased to see you?" he said.

"Mr. W. H., all happiness," said Dennis involuntarily.

"Pardon me?"

"I am the Happier Hunting Ground," said Dennis.

"Yes, come along in."

Dennis opened the back of the wagon and took out an aluminium container. "Will this be large enough?"

"Plenty."

They entered the house. A lady, also dressed for the evening in a long, low gown and a diamond tiara, sat in the hall with a glass in her hand.

"This has been a terrible experience for Mrs. Heinkel."

"I don't want to see him. I don't want to speak of it," said the lady.

"The Happier Hunting Ground assumes all responsibility," said Dennis.

"This way," said Mr. Heinkel. "In the pantry."

The Sealyham lay on the draining board beside the sink. Dennis lifted it into the container.

"Perhaps you wouldn't mind taking a hand?"

Together he and Mr. Heinkel carried their load to the wagon.

"Shall we discuss arrangements now, or would you prefer to call in the morning?"

"I'm a pretty busy man mornings," said Mr. Heinkel. "Come into the study."

There was a tray on the desk. They helped themselves to whisky.

"I have our brochure here setting out our service. Were you thinking of interment or incineration?"

"Pardon me?"

"Buried or burned?"

"Burned, I guess."

"I have some photographs here of various styles of urn."

"The best will be good enough."

"Would you require a niche in our columbarium or do you prefer to keep the remains at home?"

"What you said first."

"And the religious rites? We have a pastor who is always pleased to assist."

"Well, Mr.—?"

"Barlow."

"Mr. Barlow, we're neither of us what you might call very church-going people, but I think on an occasion like this Mrs. Heinkel would want all the comfort you can offer."

"Our Grade A service includes several unique features. At the moment of committal, a white dove, symbolizing the deceased's soul, is liberated over the crematorium."

"Yes," said Mr. Heinkel, "I reckon Mrs. Heinkel would appreciate the dove."

"And every anniversary a card of remembrance is mailed without further charge. It reads: *Your little Arthur is thinking of you in heaven today and wagging his tail.*"

"That's a very beautiful thought, Mr. Barlow."

"Then if you will just sign the order . . ."

Mrs. Heinkel bowed gravely to him as he passed through the hall. Mr. Heinkel accompanied him to the door of his car. "It has been a great pleasure to make your acquaintance, Mr. Barlow. You have certainly relieved me of a great responsibility."

"That is what the Happier Hunting Ground aims to do," said Dennis, and drove away.

At the administrative building, he carried the dog to the refrigerator. It was a capacious chamber, already occupied by two or three other small cadavers. Next to a Siamese cat stood a tin of fruit juice and a plate of sandwiches. Dennis took his supper into the reception-room, and, as he ate it, resumed his interrupted reading.

Two

EEKS PASSED, THE RAIN CAME, INVITATIONS dwindled and ceased. Dennis Barlow was happy in his work. Artists are by nature versatile and precise; they only repine when involved with the monotonous and the makeshift. Dennis had observed this during the recent war; a poetic friend of his in the Grenadiers was an enthusiast to the end, while he himself fretted almost to death as a wingless officer in Transport Command.

He had been dealing with Air Priorities at an Italian port when his first, his only book came out. England was no nest of singing-birds in that decade; lamas scanned the snows in vain for a reincarnation of Rupert Brooke. Dennis's poems, appearing among the buzz-bombs and the jaunty, deeply depressing publications of His Majesty's Stationery Office, achieved undesignedly something of the effect of the resistance Press of occupied Europe. They were extravagantly praised and but for the paper restrictions would have sold like a novel. On the day the *Sunday Times* reached Caserta with a two-column review, Dennis was offered the post of personal assistant to an Air Marshal. He sulkily declined, remained in "Priorities" and was presented in his absence with half a dozen literary prizes. On his discharge he came to Hollywood to help write the life of Shelley for the films.

There in the Megalopolitan studios he found repro-
duced, and enhanced by the nervous agitation endemic to
the place, all the gross futility of service life. He repined,
despaired, fled.

And now he was content; adept in a worthy trade, giving
satisfaction to Mr. Schultz, keeping Miss Poski guessing. For
the first time he knew what it was to "explore an avenue"; his
way was narrow but it was dignified and umbrageous and it
led to limitless distances.

Not all his customers were as open-handed and
tractable as the Heinkels. Some boggled at a ten-dollar
burial, others had their pets embalmed and then went East
and forgot them; one after filling half the ice-box for over
a week with a dead she-bear changed her mind and called
in the taxidermist. These were the dark days, to be set
against the ritualistic, almost orgiastic cremation of a non-
sectarian chimpanzee and the burial of a canary over whose
tiny grave a squad of Marine buglers had sounded Taps. It is
forbidden by Californian law to scatter human remains from
an aeroplane, but the sky is free to the animal world and on
one occasion it fell to Dennis to commit the ashes of a tabby-
cat to the slip-stream over Sunset Boulevard. That day he
was photographed for the local paper and his social ruin con-
summated. But he was complacent. His poem led a snakes-
and-ladders existence of composition and excision but it
continued just perceptibly to grow. Mr. Schultz raised his
wages. The scars of adolescence healed. There at the quiet
limit of the world he experienced a tranquil joy such as he
had known only once before, one glorious early Eastertide

when, honourably lamed in a house-match, he had lain in bed and heard below the sanatorium windows the school marching out for a field-day.

But while Dennis prospered, things were not well with Sir Francis. The old man was losing his equanimity. He fidgeted with his food and shuffled sleeplessly about the veranda in the silent hour of dawn. Juanita del Pablo was taking unkindly to her translation and, powerless to strike the great, was rending her old friend. Sir Francis confided his growing troubles to Dennis.

Juanita's agent was pressing the metaphysical point; did his client exist? Could you legally bind her to annihilate herself? Could you come to any agreement with her before she had acquired the ordinary marks of identity? Sir Francis was charged with the metamorphosis. How lightly, ten years before, he had brought her into existence—the dynamite-bearing Maenad of the Bilbao water-front! With what leaden effort did he now search the nomenclature of Celtic mythology and write the new life-story—a romance of the Mountains of Mourne, of the bare-foot child whom the peasants spoke of as a fairies' changeling, the confidante of leprechauns, the rough-and-tumble tomboy who pushed the moke out of the cabin and dodged the English tourists among rocks and water-falls! He read it aloud to Dennis and knew it was no good.

He read it aloud in conference, before the now nameless actress, her agent and solicitor; there were also present the Megalopolitan Directors of Law, Publicity, Personality and International Relations. In all his career in Hollywood Sir

Francis had never been in a single assembly with so many luminaries of the Grand Sanhedrin of the Corporation. They turned down his story without debate.

"Take a week at home, Frank," said the Director of Personality. "Try to work out a new slant. Or maybe you feel kind of allergic to the assignment?"

"No," said Sir Francis feebly. "No, not at all. This conference has been most helpful. I know now what you gentlemen require. I'm sure I shall have no further difficulty."

"Always very pleased to look over anything you cook up," said the Director of International Relations. But when the door closed behind him, the great men looked at one another and shook their heads.

"Just another has-been," said the Director of Personality.

"There's a cousin of my wife's just arrived," said the Director of Publicity. "Maybe I'd better give him a try-out on the job."

"Yes, Sam," they all said, "have your wife's cousin look it over."

After that Sir Francis remained at home and for several days his secretary came out daily to take dictation. He footled with a new name for Juanita and a new life-story: Kathleen FitzBourke the toast of the Galway Blazers; the falling light among the banks and walls of that stiff country and Kathleen FitzBourke alone with hounds, far from the crumbling towers of FitzBourke Castle . . . Then there came a day when his secretary failed to arrive. He telephoned to the studio. The call was switched from one administrative office to another until eventually a voice said: "Yes, Sir Francis, that is quite in order. Miss Mavrocordato has been transferred to the Catering Department."

"Well, I must have somebody."

"I'm not sure we have anyone available right now, Sir Francis."

"I see. Well, it is very inconvenient but I'll have to come down and finish the work I am doing in the studio. Will you have a car sent for me?"

"I'll put you through to Mr. Van Gluck."

Again the call went to and fro like a shuttlecock until finally a voice said: "Transportation Captain. No, Sir Francis, I'm sorry, we don't have a studio automobile right here right now."

Already feeling the mantle of Lear about his shoulders Sir Francis took a taxi to the studio. He nodded to the girl at the desk with something less than his usual urbanity.

"Good morning, Sir Francis," she said. "Can I help you?"

"No, thank you."

"There isn't anyone particular you were looking for?"

"No one."

The elevator-girl looked inquiringly at him. "Going up?"

"Third floor, of course."

He walked down the familiar featureless corridor, opened the familiar door and stopped abruptly. A stranger sat at the desk.

"I'm so sorry," said Sir Francis. "Stupid of me. Never done that before." He backed out and shut the door. Then he studied it. It was his number. He had made no mistake. But in the slot which had borne his name for twelve years—ever

since he came to this department from the script-writers'—
there was now a card typewritten with the name "Lorenzo
Medici." He opened the door again. "I say," he said. "There
must be some mistake."

"Maybe there is too," said Mr. Medici, cheerfully. "Everything seems kinda screwy around here. I've spent half the
morning clearing junk out of this room. Piles of stuff, just
like someone had been living here—bottles of medicine,
books, photographs, kids' games. Seems it belonged to some
old Britisher who's just kicked off."

"I am that Britisher and I have not kicked off."

"Mighty glad to hear it. Hope there wasn't anything you
valued in the junk. Maybe it's still around somewhere."

"I must go and see Otto Baumbein."

"He's screwy too but I don't figure he'll know anything
about the junk. I just pushed it out in the passage. Maybe
some janitor . . ."

Sir Francis went down the passage to the office of the assistant director. "Mr. Baumbein is in conference right now.
Shall I have him call you?"

"I'll wait."

He sat in the outer office where two typists enjoyed long,
intimately amorous telephone conversations. At last Mr.
Baumbein came out. "Why, Frank," he said. "Mighty nice of
you to look us up. I appreciate that. I do really. Come again.
Come often, Frank."

"I wanted to talk to you, Otto."

"Well, I'm rather busy right now, Frank. How say I give
you a ring next week sometime?"

"I've just found a Mr. Medici in my office."

"Why, yes, Frank. Only he says it 'Medissy,' like that; how you said it kinda sounds like a wop and Mr. Medici is a very fine young man with a very, very fine and wonderful record, Frank, who I'd be proud to have you meet."

"Then where do I work?"

"Well now see here, Frank, that's a thing I want very much to talk to you about but I haven't the time right now. I haven't the time, have I, dear?"

"No, Mr. Baumbein," said one of the secretaries. "You certainly haven't the time."

"You see. I just haven't the time. I know what, dear, try fix it for Sir Francis to see Mr. Erikson. I know Mr. Erikson would greatly appreciate it."

So Sir Francis saw Mr. Erikson, Mr. Baumbein's immediate superior, and from him learned in blunt Nordic terms what he had already in the last hour darkly surmised; that his long service with Megalopolitan Pictures Inc. had come to an end.

"It would have been civil to tell me," said Sir Francis.

"The letter is on its way. Things get hung up sometimes, as you know; so many different departments have to give their O.K.—the Legal Branch, Finance, Labour Disputes Section. But I don't anticipate any trouble in your case. Luckily you aren't a Union man. Now and then the Big Three make objections about waste of manpower—when we bring someone from Europe or China or somewhere and then fire him in a week. But that doesn't arise in your case. You've had a record run. Just on twenty-five

years, isn't it? There's not even any provision in your contract for repatriation. Your Termination ought to whip
right through."

Sir Francis left Mr. Erikson and made his way out of the
great hive. It was called the Wilbur K. Lutit Memorial Block
and had not been built when Sir Francis first came to Hollywood. Wilbur K. Lutit had been alive then; had, indeed, once
pudgily shaken his hand. Sir Francis had watched the edifice
rise and had had an honourable if not illustrious place at its
dedication. He had seen the rooms filled and refilled, the
name plates change on the doors. He had seen arrivals and
departures, Mr. Erikson and Mr. Baumbein coming, others,
whose names now escaped him, going. He remembered poor
Leo who had fallen from great heights to die with his bill un-
paid in the Tents of Kedar Hotel.

"Did you find who you were looking for?" asked the girl
at the desk as he made his way out into the sunshine.

<hr/>

2

Turf does not prosper in Southern California and the Hollywood ground did not permit the larger refinements of
cricket. The game indeed was fitfully played by some of the
junior members, but for the majority it formed as small a part
in their interests as do fishmongering or cordwaining to the
Livery Companies of the City of London. For these the club
was the symbol of their englishry. Here they collected sub-
scriptions for the Red Cross and talked at their ease, mali-
ciously, out of the hearing of their alien employers and

protectors. There on the day following Sir Francis Hinsley's unexpected death the expatriates repaired as though summoned by tocsin.

"Young Barlow found him."

"Barlow of Megalo?"

"He used to be at Megalo's. His contract wasn't renewed. Since then . . ."

"Yes, I heard. That was a shocking business."

"I never knew Sir Francis. He was rather before my time. Does anyone know why he did it?"

"*His* contract wasn't renewed."

They were words of ill-omen to all that assembled company, words never spoken without the furtive touching of wood or crossing of fingers; unholy words best left unsaid. To each of them was given a span of life between the signature of the contract and its expiration; beyond that lay the vast unknowable.

"Where is Sir Ambrose? He's sure to come this evening."

He came at length and it was noted that he already wore a band of crêpe on his Coldstream blazer. Late as it was he accepted a cup of tea, snuffed the air of suspense that filled the pavilion to stifling, and spoke:

"No doubt you've all heard of this ghastly business of old Frank?"

A murmur.

"He fell on bad days at the end. I don't suppose there's anyone in Hollywood now except myself who remembers him in his prime. He did yeoman service."

"He was a scholar and a gentleman."

"Exactly. He was one of the first Englishmen of distinction to go into motion-pictures. You might say he laid the foundations on which I—on which we all have built. He was our first ambassador."

"I really think that Megalo might have kept him on. They wouldn't notice his salary. In the course of nature he couldn't have cost them much more."

"People live to a great age in this place."

"Oh, it wasn't that," said Sir Ambrose. "There were other reasons." He paused. Then the false and fruity tones continued: "I think I had better tell you because it is a thing which has a bearing on all our lives here. I don't think many of you visited old Frank in recent years. I did. I make a point of keeping up with all the English out here. Well, as you may know, he had taken in a young Englishman named Dennis Barlow." The cricketers looked at one another, some knowingly, others in surmise. "Now I don't want to say a word against Barlow. He came out here with a high reputation as a poet. He just hasn't made good, I'm afraid. That is nothing to condemn him for. This is a hard testing ground. Only the best survive. Barlow failed. As soon as I heard of it I went to see him. I advised him as bluntly as I could to clear out. I thought it my duty to you all. We don't want any poor Englishmen hanging around Hollywood. I told him as much, frankly and fairly, as one Englishman to another.

"Well, I think most of you know what his answer was. *He took a job at the pets' cemetery.*

"In Africa, if a white man is disgracing himself and letting down his people the authorities pack him off home. We haven't any such rights here, unfortunately. The trouble is we all suffer for the folly of one. Do you suppose Megalo would have sacked poor Frank in other circumstances? But when they saw him sharing a house with a fellow who worked in the pets' cemetery . . . Well, I ask you! You all know the form out here almost as well as I do. I've nothing to say against our American colleagues. They're as fine a set of chaps as you'll find anywhere and they've created the finest industry in the world. They have their standards—that's all. Who's to blame 'em? In a world of competition people are taken at their face value. Everything depends on reputation—'face' as they say out East. Lose that and you lose everything. Frank lost face. I will say no more.

"Personally I'm sorry for young Barlow. I wouldn't stand in his shoes today. I've just come from seeing the lad. I thought it was the decent thing. I hope any of you who come across him will remember that his chief fault was inexperience. He wouldn't be guided. However . . .

"I've left all the preliminary arrangements in his hands. He's going up to Whispering Glades as soon as the police hand over the remains. Give him something to do, to take his mind off it, I thought.

"This is an occasion when we've all got to show the flag. We may have to put our hands in our pockets—I don't suppose old Frank has left much—but it will be money well spent if it puts the British colony right in the eyes of the industry. I called Washington and asked them to send the Ambassador to the funeral, but it doesn't seem they can manage it. I'll try again. It would make a lot of difference. In any case I don't think the studios will keep away if they know *we* are solid . . ."

As he spoke the sun sank below the bushy western hillside. The sky was still bright but a deep shadow crept over the tough and ragged grass of the cricket field, bringing with it a sharp chill.

THREE

D ENNIS WAS A YOUNG MAN OF SENSIBILITY RATHER
than of sentiment. He had lived his twenty-eight
years at arm's length from violence, but he came of
a generation which enjoys a vicarious intimacy with death.
Never, it so happened, had he seen a human corpse until that
morning when, returning tired from night duty, he found his
host strung to the rafters. The spectacle had been rude and
momentarily unnerving; perhaps it had left a scar somewhere
out of sight in his subconscious mind. But his reason accepted the event as part of the established order. Others in
gentler ages had had their lives changed by such a revelation;
to Dennis it was the kind of thing to be expected in the world
he knew and, as he drove to Whispering Glades, his con-
scious mind was pleasantly exhilarated and full of curiosity.

Times without number since he first came to Hollywood
he had heard the name of that great necropolis on the lips of
others; he had read it in the local news-sheets when some
more than usually illustrious body was given more than usually splendid honours or some new acquisition was made to
its collected masterpieces of contemporary art. Of recent
weeks his interest had been livelier and more technical for it
was in humble emulation of its great neighbour that the Happier Hunting Ground was planned. The language he daily

spoke in his new trade was a *patois* derived from that high pure source. More than once Mr. Schultz had exultantly exclaimed after one of his performances: "It was worthy of Whispering Glades." As a missionary priest making his first pilgrimage to the Vatican, as a paramount chief of equatorial Africa mounting the Eiffel Tower, Dennis Barlow, poet and pets' mortician, drove through the Golden Gates.

They were vast, the largest in the world, and freshly regilt. A notice proclaimed the inferior dimensions of their Old World rivals. Beyond them lay a semi-circle of golden yew, a wide gravel roadway and an island of mown turf on which stood a singular and massive wall of marble sculptured in the form of an open book. Here, in letters a foot high, was incised:

> *The Dream*
>   *Behold I dreamed a dream and I saw a New Earth sacred to HAPPINESS. There amid all that Nature and Art could offer to elevate the Soul of Man I saw the Happy Resting Place of Countless Loved Ones. And I saw the Waiting Ones who still stood at the brink of that narrow stream that now separated them from those who had gone before. Young and old, they were happy too. Happy in Beauty, Happy in the certain knowledge that their Loved Ones were very near, in Beauty and Happiness such as the earth cannot give.*
>   *I heard a voice say: "Do this."*
>   *And behold I awoke and in the Light and Promise of my DREAM I made WHISPERING GLADES.*
>   *ENTER STRANGER and BE HAPPY.*

And below, in vast cursive facsimile, the signature:

WILBUR KENWORTHY, THE DREAMER.

A modest wooden signboard beside it read: *Prices on enquiry at Administrative Building. Drive straight on.*

Dennis drove on through green parkland and presently came in sight of what in England he would have taken for the country seat of an Edwardian financier. It was black and white, timbered and gabled, with twisting brick chimneys and wrought iron wind-vanes. He left his car among a dozen others and proceeded on foot through a box walk, past a sunken herb garden, a sun-dial, a bird-bath and fountain, a rustic seat and a pigeon-cote. Music rose softly all round him, the subdued notes of the "Hindu Love-song" relayed from an organ through countless amplifiers concealed about the garden.

When as a newcomer to the Megalopolitan Studios he first toured the lots, it had taxed his imagination to realize that those solid-seeming streets and squares of every period and climate were in fact plaster façades whose backs revealed the structure of bill-boardings. Here the illusion was quite otherwise. Only with an effort could Dennis believe that the building before him was three-dimensional and permanent; but here, as everywhere in Whispering Glades, failing credulity was fortified by the painted word.

This perfect replica of an old English Manor, a notice said, *like all the buildings of Whispering Glades, is constructed throughout of Grade A steel and concrete with foundations ex-*

tending into solid rock. It is certified proof against fire, earthquake and—Their name liveth for evermore who record it in Whispering Glades.

At the blank patch a signwriter was even then at work and Dennis, pausing to study it, discerned the ghost of the words "high explosive" freshly obliterated and the outlines of "nuclear fission" about to be filled in as substitute.

Followed by music he stepped as it were from garden to garden for the approach to the offices lay through a florist's shop. Here one young lady was spraying scent over a stall of lilac while a second was talking on the telephone: ". . . Oh, Mrs. Bogolov, I'm really sorry but it's just one of the things that Whispering Glades does not do. The Dreamer does not approve of wreaths or crosses. We just arrange the flowers in their own natural beauty. It's one of the Dreamer's own ideas. I'm sure Mr. Bogolov would prefer it himself. Won't you just leave it to us, Mrs. Bogolov? You tell us what you want to spend and we will do the rest. I'm sure you will be more than satisfied. Thank you, Mrs. Bogolov, it's a pleasure . . ."

Dennis passed through and opening the door marked *Enquiries* found himself in a raftered banqueting hall. The "Hindu Love-song" was here also, gently discoursed from the dark oak panelling. A young lady rose from a group of her fellows to welcome him, one of that new race of exquisite, amiable, efficient young ladies whom he had met everywhere in the United States. She wore a white smock and over her sharply supported left breast was embroidered the words, *Mortuary Hostess.*

"Can I help you in any way?"

"I came to arrange about a funeral."

"Is it for yourself?"

"Certainly not. Do I look so moribund?"

"Pardon me?"

"Do I look as if I were about to die?"

"Why, no. Only many of our friends like to make Before Need Arrangements. Will you come this way?"

She led him from the hall into a soft passage. The décor here was Georgian. The "Hindu Love-song" came to its end and was succeeded by the voice of a nightingale. In a little chintzy parlour he and his hostess sat down to make their arrangements.

"I must first record the Essential Data."

He told her his name and Sir Francis's.

"Now, Mr. Barlow, what had you in mind? Embalmment of course, and after that incineration or not, according to taste. Our crematory is on scientific principles, the heat is so intense that all inessentials are volatilized. Some people did not like the thought that ashes of the casket and clothing were mixed with the Loved One's. Normal disposal is by in-humement, entombment, inurnment or immurement, but many people just lately prefer insarcophagusment. That is *very* individual. The casket is placed inside a sealed sarcophagus, marble or bronze, and rests permanently above ground in a niche in the mausoleum, with or without a personal stained-glass window above. That, of course, is for those with whom price is not a primary consideration."

"We want my friend buried."

"This is not your first visit to Whispering Glades?"

"Yes."

"Then let me explain the Dream. The Park is zoned. Each zone has its own name and appropriate Work of Art. Zones of course vary in price and within the zones the prices vary according to their proximity to the Work of Art. We have single sites as low as fifty dollars. That is in Pilgrims' Rest, a zone we are just developing behind the Crematory fuel dump. The most costly are those on Lake Isle. They range about a thousand dollars. Then there is Lovers' Nest, zoned about a very, very beautiful marble replica of Rodin's famous statue, the Kiss. We have double plots there at seven hundred and fifty dollars the pair. Was your Loved One married?"

"No."

"What was his business?"

"He was a writer."

"Ah, then Poets' Corner would be the place for him. We have many of our foremost literary names there, either in person or as Before Need reservations. You are no doubt acquainted with the works of Amelia Bergson?"

"I know of them."

"We sold Miss Bergson a Before Need reservation only yesterday, under the statue of the prominent Greek poet Homer. I could put your friend right next to her. But perhaps you would like to see the zone before deciding?"

"I want to see everything."

"There certainly is plenty to see. I'll have one of our guides take you round just as soon as we have all the Essential Data, Mr. Barlow. Was your Loved One of any special religion?"

"An Agnostic."

"We have two non-sectarian churches in the Park and a number of non-sectarian pastors. Jews and Catholics seem to prefer to make their own arrangements."

"I believe Sir Ambrose Abercrombie is planning a special service."

"Oh, was your Loved One in films, Mr. Barlow? In that case he ought to be in Shadowland."

"I think he would prefer to be with Homer and Miss Bergson."

"Then the University Church would be most convenient. We like to save the Waiting Ones a long procession. I presume the Loved One was Caucasian?"

"No, why did you think that? He was purely English."

"English are purely Caucasian, Mr. Barlow. This is a restricted park. The Dreamer has made that rule for the sake of the Waiting Ones. In their time of trial they prefer to be with their own people."

"I think I understand. Well, let me assure you Sir Francis was quite white."

As he said this there came vividly into Dennis's mind that image which lurked there, seldom out of sight for long; the sack or body suspended and the face above it with eyes red and horribly starting from their sockets, the cheeks mottled in indigo like the marbled end-papers of a ledger and the tongue swollen and protruding like an end of black sausage.

"Let us now decide on the casket."

They went to the show-rooms where stood coffins of every shape and material; the nightingale still sang in the cornice.

"The two-piece lid is most popular for gentlemen Loved Ones. Only the upper part is then exposed to view."

"Exposed to view?"

"Yes, when the Waiting Ones come to take leave."

"But, I say, I don't think that will quite do. I've seen him. He's terribly disfigured, you know."

"If there are any special little difficulties in the case you must mention them to our cosmeticians. You will be seeing one of them before you leave. They have never failed yet."

Dennis made no hasty choice. He studied all that was for sale; even the simplest of these coffins, he humbly recognized, outshone the most gorgeous product of the Happier Hunting Ground and when he approached the two thousand dollar level—and these were not the costliest—he felt himself in the Egypt of the Pharaohs. At length he decided on a massive chest of walnut with bronze enrichments and an interior of quilted satin. Its lid, as recommended, was in two parts.

"You are sure that they will be able to make him presentable?"

"We had a Loved One last month who was found drowned. He had been in the sea a month and they only identified him by his wrist-watch. They fixed that stiff," said the hostess disconcertingly lapsing from the high diction she had hitherto employed, "so he looked like it was his wedding day. The boys up there surely know their job. Why if he'd sat on an atom bomb, they'd make him presentable."

"That's very comforting."

"I'll say it is." And then slipping on her professional manner again as though it were a pair of glasses, she resumed. "How will the Loved One be attired? We have our own tailoring section. Sometimes after a very long illness there are not suitable clothes available and sometimes the Waiting Ones think it a waste of a good suit. You see we can fit a Loved One out very reasonably as a casket-suit does not have to be designed for hard wear and in cases where only the upper part is exposed for leave-taking there is no need for more than jacket and vest. Something dark is best to set off the flowers."

Dennis was entirely fascinated. At length he said: "Sir Francis was not much of a dandy. I doubt of his having anything quite suitable for casket wear. But in Europe, I think, we usually employ a shroud."

"Oh, we have shrouds too. I'll show you some."

The hostess led him to a set of sliding shelves like a sacristy chest where vestments are stored, and drawing one out revealed a garment such as Dennis had never seen before. Observing his interest she held it up for his closer inspection. It was in appearance like a suit of clothes, buttoned in front but open down the back; the sleeves hung loose, open at the seam; half an inch of linen appeared at the cuff and the V of the waistcoat was similarly filled; a knotted bow-tie emerged from the opening of a collar which also lay as though slit from behind. It was the apotheosis of the "dickey."

"A speciality of our own," she said, "though it is now widely imitated. The idea came from the quick-change artists of vaudeville. It enables one to dress the Loved One without disturbing the pose."

"Most remarkable. I believe that is just the article we require."

"With or without trousers?"

"What precisely is the advantage of trousers?"

"For Slumber-Room wear. It depends whether you wish the leave-taking to be on the chaise-longue or in the casket."

"Perhaps I had better see the Slumber Room before deciding."

"You're welcome."

She led him out to the hall and up a staircase. The nightingale had now given place to the organ and strains of Handel followed them to the Slumber Floor. Here she asked a colleague, "Which room have we free?"

"Only Daffodil."

"This way, Mr. Barlow."

They passed many closed doors of pickled oak until at length she opened one and stood aside for him to enter. He found a little room, brightly furnished and papered. It might have been part of a luxurious modern country club in all its features save one. Bowls of flowers stood disposed about a chintz sofa and on the sofa lay what seemed to be the wax effigy of an elderly woman dressed as though for an evening party. Her white gloved hands held a bouquet and on her nose glittered a pair of rimless pince-nez.

"Oh," said his guide, "how foolish of me. We've come into Primrose by mistake. This," she added superfluously, "is occupied."

"Yes."

"The leave-taking is not till the afternoon but we had better go before one of the cosmeticians finds us. They like to make a few final adjustments before Waiting Ones are admitted. Still it gives you an idea of the chaise-longue arrangement. We usually recommend the casket half-exposure for gentlemen because the legs never look so well."

She led him out.

"Will there be many for the leave-taking?"

"Yes, I rather think so, a great many."

"Then you had better have a suite with an ante-room. The Orchid Room is the best. Shall I make a reservation for that?"

"Yes, do."

"And the half-exposure in the casket, not the chaise-longue?"

"Not the chaise-longue."

She led him back towards the reception-room.

"It may seem a little strange to you, Mr. Barlow, coming on a Loved One unexpectedly in that way."

"I confess it did a little."

"You will find it quite different on the day. The leave-taking is a very, very great source of consolation. Often the Waiting Ones last saw their Loved Ones on a bed of pain surrounded by all the gruesome concomitants of the sick room or the hospital. Here they see them as they knew them in buoyant life, transfigured with peace and happiness. At the funeral they have time only for a last look as they file past. Here in the Slumber Room they can stand as long as they like photographing a last beautiful memory on the mind."

She spoke, he observed, partly by the book, in the words of the Dreamer, partly in her own brisk language. They were

back in the reception-room now and she spoke briskly.
"Well, I guess I've got all I want out of you, Mr. Barlow, except your signature to the order and a deposit."

Dennis had come prepared for this. It was part of the
Happier Hunting Ground procedure. He paid her five hundred dollars and took her receipt.

"Now one of our cosmeticians is waiting to see you, and
get *her* Essential Data, but before we part, may I interest you
in our Before Need Provision Arrangements?"

"Everything about Whispering Glades interests me pro-
foundly, but that aspect, perhaps, less than others."

"The benefits of the plan are twofold"—she was speaking
by the book now with a vengeance—"financial and psycho-
logical. You, Mr. Barlow, are now approaching your opti-
mum earning phase. You are no doubt making provision of
many kinds for your future—investments, insurance policies
and so forth. You plan to spend your declining days in secu-
rity but have you considered what burdens you may not be
piling up for those you leave behind? Last month, Mr. Barlow, a husband and wife were here consulting us about Before Need Provision. They were prominent citizens in the
prime of life with two daughters just budding into woman-
hood. They heard all particulars, they were impressed and
said they would return in a few days to complete arrangements. Only next day those two passed on, Mr. Barlow, in an
automobile accident, and instead of them there came two distraught orphans to ask what arrangements their parents had
made. We were obliged to inform them that *no* arrangements
had been made. In the hour of their greatest need those chil-

dren were left comfortless. How different it would have been had we been able to say to them: 'Welcome to all the Happiness of Whispering Glades.' "

"Yes, but you know I haven't any children. Besides I am a foreigner. I have no intention of dying here."

"Mr. Barlow, you are afraid of death."

"No, I assure you."

"It is a natural instinct, Mr. Barlow, to shrink from the unknown. But if you discuss it openly and frankly you remove morbid reflexions. That is one of the things the psychoanalysts have taught us. Bring your dark fears into the light of the common day of the common man, Mr. Barlow. Realize that death is not a private tragedy of your own but the general lot of man. As Hamlet so beautifully writes: 'Know that death is common; all that live must die.' Perhaps you think it morbid and even dangerous to give thought to this subject, Mr. Barlow, the contrary has been proved by scientific investigation. Many people let their vital energy lag prematurely and their earning capacity diminish simply through fear of death. By removing that fear they actually increase their expectation of life. Choose now, at leisure and in health, the form of final preparation you require, pay for it while you are best able to do so, shed all anxiety. Pass the buck, Mr. Barlow; Whispering Glades can take it."

"I will give the matter every consideration."

"I'll leave our brochure with you. And now I must hand you over to the cosmetician."

She left the room and Dennis at once forgot everything about her. He had seen her before everywhere. American

mothers, Dennis reflected, presumably knew their daughters
apart, as the Chinese were said subtly to distinguish one
from another of their seemingly uniform race, but to the European eye the Mortuary Hostess was one with all her sisters
of the air-liners and the reception-desks, one with Miss
Poski at the Happier Hunting Ground. She was the standard
product. A man could leave such a girl in a delicatessen shop
in New York, fly three thousand miles and find her again in
the cigar stall at San Francisco, just as he would find his
favourite comic strip in the local paper; and she would croon
the same words to him in moments of endearment and express the same views and preferences in moments of social
discourse. She was convenient; but Dennis came of an earlier civilization with sharper needs. He sought the intangi-
ble, the veiled face in the fog, the silhouette at the lighted
doorway, the secret graces of a body which hid itself under
formal velvet. He did not covet the spoils of this rich conti-
nent, the sprawling limbs of the swimming-pool, the wide-
open painted eyes and mouths under the arc-lamps. But the
girl who now entered was unique. Not indefinably; the appropriate distinguishing epithet leapt to Dennis's mind the
moment he saw her: sole Eve in a bustling hygienic Eden,
this girl was a decadent.

　　She wore the white livery of her calling; she entered the
room, sat at the table and poised her fountain pen with the
same professional assurance as her predecessor's, but she was
what Dennis had vainly sought during a lonely year of exile.

　　Her hair was dark and straight, her brows wide, her skin
transparent and untarnished by sun. Her lips were artificially

tinctured, no doubt, but not coated like her sisters' and clogged in all their delicate pores with crimson grease; they seemed to promise instead an unmeasured range of sensual converse. Her full-face was oval, her profile pure and classical and light. Her eyes greenish and remote, with a rich glint of lunacy.

Dennis held his breath. When the girl spoke it was briskly and prosaically.

"What did your Loved One pass on from?" she asked.

"He hanged himself."

"Was the face much disfigured?"

"Hideously."

"That is quite usual. Mr. Joyboy will probably take him in hand personally. It is a question of touch, you see, massaging the blood from the congested areas. Mr. Joyboy has very wonderful hands."

"And what do you do?"

"Hair, skin and nails and I brief the embalmers for expression and pose. Have you brought any photographs of your Loved One? They are the greatest help in re-creating personality. Was he a very cheerful old gentleman?"

"No, rather the reverse."

"Shall I put him down as serene and philosophical or judicial and determined?"

"I think the former."

"It is the hardest of all expressions to fix, but Mr. Joyboy makes it his speciality—that and the joyful smile for children. Did the Loved One wear his own hair? And the normal complexion? We usually classify them as rural, athletic and scholarly—that is to say red, brown or white. Scholarly? And spectacles? A monocle. They are always a difficulty because Mr. Joyboy likes to incline the head slightly to give a more natural pose. Pince-nez and monocles are difficult to keep in place once the flesh has firmed. Also of course the monocle looks less natural when the eye is closed. Did you particularly wish to feature it?"

"No, let us eliminate the monocle."

"Just as you wish, Mr. Barlow. Of course, Mr. Joyboy *can* fix it."

"No. I think your point about the eye being closed is decisive."

"Very well. Did the Loved One pass over with a rope?"

"Braces. What you call suspenders."

"That should be quite easy to deal with. Sometimes there is a permanent line left. We had a Loved One last month who passed over with electric cord. Even Mr. Joyboy could do nothing with that. We had to wind a scarf right up to the chin. But suspenders should come out quite satisfactorily."

"You have a great regard for Mr. Joyboy, I notice."

"He is a true artist, Mr. Barlow. I can say no more."

"You enjoy your work?"

"I regard it as a very, very great privilege, Mr. Barlow."

"Have you been at it long?"

Normally, Dennis had found, the people of the United States were slow to resent curiosity about their commercial careers. This cosmetician, however, seemed to draw another thickness of veil between herself and her interlocutor.

"Eighteen months," she said briefly. "And now I have almost come to the end of my questions. Is there any individual trait you would like portrayed? Sometimes for instance the Waiting Ones like to see a pipe in the Loved One's mouth. Or anything special in his hands? In the case of children we usually give them a toy to hold. Is there anything specially characteristic of your Loved One? Many like a musical instrument. One lady made her leave-taking holding a telephone."

"No, I don't think that would be suitable."

"Just flowers? One further point—dentures. Was he wearing them when he passed on?"

"I really don't know."

"Will you try and find out? Often they disappear at the police mortuary and it causes great extra work for Mr. Joyboy. Loved Ones who pass over by their own hand *usually* wear their dentures."

"I'll look round his room and if I don't see them I'll mention it to the police."

"Thank you very much, Mr. Barlow. Well, that completes my Essential Data. It has been a pleasure to make your acquaintance."

"When shall I see you again?"

"The day after tomorrow. You had better come a little before the leave-taking to see that everything is as you wish."

"Who shall I ask for?"

"Just say the cosmetician of the Orchid Room."

"No name?"

"No name is necessary."

She left him and the forgotten hostess returned.

"Mr. Barlow, I have the Zone Guide ready to take you to the site."

Dennis awoke from a deep abstraction. "Oh, I'll take the site on trust," he said. "To tell you the truth I think I've seen enough for one day."

FOUR

———————※·※———————

DENNIS SOUGHT AND OBTAINED LEAVE OF ABSENCE from the Happier Hunting Ground for the funeral and its preliminaries. Mr. Schultz did not give it readily. He could ill spare Dennis; more motor cars were coming off the assembly-lines, more drivers appearing on the roads and more pets in the mortuary; there was an outbreak of food poisoning in Pasadena. The ice-box was packed and the crematorium fires blazed early and late.

"It is really very valuable experience for me, Mr. Schultz," Dennis said, seeking to extenuate the reproach of desertion. "I see a great deal of the methods of Whispering Glades and am picking up all kinds of ideas we might introduce here."

"What for you want new ideas?" asked Mr. Schultz. "Cheaper fuel, cheaper wages, harder work, that is all the new ideas I want. Look, Mr. Barlow, we got all of the trade of the coast. There's nothing in our class between San Francisco and the Mexican border. Do we get people to pay five thousand dollars for a pet's funeral? How many pay five hundred? Not two in a month. What do most of our clients say? 'Burn him up cheap, Mr. Schultz, just so the City don't have him and make me a shame.' Or else it's a fifty-dollar grave and headstone inclusive of collection. There ain't the demand for fancy stuff since the war, Mr. Barlow. Folks pretend to love their pets, talk to them like they was children, along comes a citizen with a new auto, floods of tears, and then it's 'Is a headstone really socially essential, Mr. Schultz?' "

"Mr. Schultz, you're jealous of Whispering Glades."

"And why wouldn't I be seeing all that dough going on relations they've hated all their lives, while the pets who've loved them and stood by them, never asked no questions, never complained, rich or poor, sickness or health, get buried anyhow like animals? Take your three days off, Mr. Barlow, only don't expect to be paid for them on account you're thinking up some fancy ideas."

The coroner caused no trouble. Dennis gave his evidence; the Whispering Glades van carried off the remains; Sir Ambrose blandly managed the press. Sir Ambrose, also, with the help of other prominent Englishmen composed the Order of the Service. Liturgy in Hollywood is the concern of the Stage rather than of the Clergy. Everyone at the Cricket Club wanted a part.

"There should be a reading from the Works," said Sir Ambrose. "I'm not sure I can lay my hand on a copy at the moment. These things disappear mysteriously when one moves house. Barlow, you are a literary chap. No doubt you can find a suitable passage. Something I'd suggest that gives one the essence of the man we knew—his love of nature, his fair-play, you know."

"Did Frank love nature or fair-play?"

"Why, he must have done. Great figure in letters and all that; honoured by the King."

"I don't ever remember seeing any of his works in the house."

"Find something, Barlow. Just some little personal scrap. Write it yourself if necessary. I expect you know his style. And, I say, come to think of it, you're a poet. Don't you think this is just the time to write something about old Frank? Something I can recite at the graveside you know. After all, damn it, you owe it to him—and to us. It isn't much to ask. We're doing all the donkey work."

"Donkey work" was the word, thought Dennis as he watched the cricketers compiling the list of invitations. There was a cleavage on this subject. A faction were in favour of keeping the party small and British, the majority headed by Sir Ambrose wished to include all the leaders of the film industry. It was no use "showing the flag" he explained if there was no one except poor old Frank to show it to. It was never in doubt who would win. Sir Ambrose had all the heavy weapons. Cards were accordingly printed in large numbers.

Dennis meanwhile searched for any traces of Sir Francis's "Works." There were few books in the bungalow and those few mostly Dennis's own. Sir Francis had given up writing before Dennis could read. He did not remember those charming books which had appeared while he lay in the cradle, books with patterned paper boards and paper labels, with often a little scribble by Lovat Fraser on the title page, fruits of a frivolous but active mind, biography, travel, criticism, poetry, drama—*belles lettres* in short. The most ambitious was *A Free Man Greets the Dawn*, half auto-biographical, a quarter political, a quarter mystical, a work which went straight to the heart of every Boots subscriber in the early twenties, and earned Sir Francis his knighthood. *A Free Man Greets the Dawn* had been out of print for years now, all its pleasant phrases unhonoured and unremembered.

When Dennis met Sir Francis in Megalopolitan studios the name Hinsley was just not unknown. There was a sonnet by him in *Poems of Today*. If asked, Dennis would have guessed that he had been killed in the Dardanelles. It was not surprising that Dennis possessed none of the Works. Nor, to any who knew Sir Francis, was it surprising that *he* did not. To the end he was the least vain of literary men and in consequence the least remembered.

Dennis searched long in vain and was contemplating a desperate sortie to the public library when he found a stained old copy of the *Apollo* preserved, Heaven knew why, in Sir Francis's handkerchief drawer. The blue cover had faded to grey, the date was February 1920. It comprised chiefly poems by women, many of them, probably, grandmothers by now. Perhaps one of these warm lyrics explained the magazine's preservation after so many years in so remote an outpost. There was, however, at the end a book review signed F. H. It dealt, Dennis noticed, with a poetess whose sonnets appeared on an earlier page. The name was now forgotten, but perhaps here, Dennis reflected, was something "near the heart of the man," something which explained his long exile; something anyway which obviated a trip to the public library . . . "This slim volume redolent of a passionate and reflective talent above the ordinary . . ." Dennis cut out the review and sent it to Sir Ambrose. Then he turned to his task of composition.

The pickled oak, the chintz, the spongey carpet and the Georgian staircase all ended sharply on the second floor. Above that lay a quarter where no layman penetrated. It was approached by elevator, an open functional cage eight feet square. On this top floor everything was tile and porcelain, linoleum and chromium. Here there were the embalming rooms with their rows of inclined china slabs, their taps and tubes and pressure pumps, their deep gutters and the heavy smell of formaldehyde. Beyond lay the cosmetic rooms with their smell of shampoo and hot hair and acetone and lavender.

An orderly wheeled the stretcher into Aimée's cubicle. It bore a figure under a sheet. Mr. Joyboy walked beside it.

"Good morning, Miss Thanatogenos."

"Good morning, Mr. Joyboy."

"Here is the strangulated Loved One for the Orchid Room."

Mr. Joyboy was the perfection of high professional manners. Before he came there had been some decline of gentility in the ascent from show-room to work-shop. There had been talk of "bodies" and "cadavers"; one jaunty young embalmer from Texas had even spoken of "the meat." That young man had gone within a week of Mr. Joyboy's appointment as Senior Mortician. That event occurred a month after Aimée Thanatogenos came to Whispering Glades as junior cosmetician. She remembered the bad old days before his arrival and gratefully recognized the serene hush which seemed by nature to surround him.

Mr. Joyboy was not a handsome man by the standards of motion-picture studios. He was tall but unathletic. There was lack of shape in his head and body, a lack of colour; he had scant eyebrows and invisible eyelashes; the eyes behind his pince-nez were pinkish-grey; his hair, though neat and scented, was sparse; his hands were fleshy; his best feature was perhaps his teeth and they though white and regular seemed rather too large for him; he was a trifle flat-footed and more than a trifle paunchy. But these physical defects were nugatory when set against his moral earnestness and the compelling charm of his softly resonant voice. It was as though there were an amplifier concealed somewhere within him and his speech came from some distant and august studio; everything he said might have been for a peak-hour listening period.

Dr. Kenworthy always bought the best and Mr. Joyboy came to Whispering Glades with a great reputation. He had taken his baccalaureate in embalming in the Middle West and for some years before his appointment to Whispering Glades had been one of the Undertaking Faculty at an historic Eastern University. He had served as Chief Social Executive at two National Morticians' Conventions. He had led a goodwill mission to the morticians of Latin America. His photograph, albeit with a somewhat ribald caption, had appeared in *Time* magazine.

Before he came there had been murmurs in the embalming room that Mr. Joyboy was a mere theorist. These were dispelled on the first morning. He had only to be seen with a corpse to be respected. It was like the appearance of a stranger in the hunting field who from the moment he is seen

in the saddle, before hounds move off, proclaims himself un-
mistakably a horseman. Mr. Joyboy was unmarried and every
girl in Whispering Glades gloated on him.

Aimée knew that her voice assumed a peculiar tone when
she spoke to him. "Was he a very difficult case, Mr. Joyboy?"

"Well, a wee bit, but I think everything has turned out satisfactorily."

He drew the sheet back and revealed the body of Sir Francis lying naked save for a new pair of white linen drawers. It
was white and slightly translucent, like weathered marble.

"Oh, Mr. Joyboy, he's beautiful."

"Yes, I fancy he has come up nicely"; he gave a little poul-
terer's pinch to the thigh. "Supple," he raised an arm and
gently bent the wrist. "I think we have two or three hours before he need take the pose. The head will have to incline
slightly to put the carotid suture in the shadow."

"But, Mr. Joyboy, you've given him the Radiant Child-
hood smile."

"Yes, don't you like it?"

"Oh, *I* like it, of course, but his Waiting One did not ask
for it."

"Miss Thanatogenos, for you the Loved Ones just naturally smile."

"Oh, Mr. Joyboy."

"It's true, Miss Thanatogenos. It seems I am just powerless to prevent it. When I am working for you there's something inside me says 'He's on his way to Miss Thanatogenos'
and my fingers just seem to take control. Haven't you noticed it?"

"Well, Mr. Joyboy, I did remark it only last week. 'All the Loved Ones that come from Mr. Joyboy lately,' I said, 'have the most beautiful smiles.' "

"All for you, Miss Thanatogenos."

No music was relayed here. The busy floor echoed with the swirling and gurgling of taps in the embalming rooms, the hum of electric dryers in the cosmetic rooms. Aimée worked like a nun, intently, serenely, methodically; first the shampoo, then the shave, then the manicure. She parted the white hair, lathered the rubbery cheeks and plied the razor; she clipped the nails and probed the cuticle. Then she drew up the wheeled table on which stood her paints and brushes and creams and concentrated breathlessly on the crucial phase of her art.

Within two hours the main task was complete. Head, neck and hands were now in full colour; somewhat harsh in tone, somewhat gross in patina, it seemed, in the penetrating light of the cosmetic room, but the *œuvre* was designed for the amber glow of the Slumber Room and the stained light of the chancel. She completed the blue stipple work round the eye-lids and stood back complacently. On soft feet Mr. Joyboy had come to her side and was looking down on her work.

"Lovely, Miss Thanatogenos," he said. "I can always trust you to carry out my intention. Did you have difficulty with the right eyelid?"

"Just a little."

"A tendency to open in the inside corner?"

"Yes, but I worked a little cream under the lid and then firmed it with No. 6."

"Excellent. I never have to tell *you* anything. We work in unison. When I send a Loved One in to you, Miss Thanatogenos, I feel as though I were speaking to you through him. Do you ever feel that at all yourself?"

"I know I'm always special proud and careful when it is one of yours, Mr. Joyboy."

"I believe you are, Miss Thanatogenos. Bless you."

Mr. Joyboy sighed. A porter's voice said: "Two more Loved Ones just coming up, Mr. Joyboy. Who are they for?"

Mr. Joyboy sighed again and went about his business.

"Mr. Vogel; are you free for the next?"

"Yes, Mr. Joyboy."

"One of them is an infant," said the porter. "Will you be taking her yourself?"

"Yes, as always. Is it a mother and child?"

The porter looked at the labels on the wrists. "No, Mr. Joyboy, no relation."

"Very well, Mr. Vogel, will you take the adult? Had they been mother and child I should have taken both, busy though I am. There is a something in individual technique—not everyone would notice it perhaps; but if I saw a pair that had been embalmed by different hands I should know at once and I should feel that the child did not properly belong to its mother; as though they had been estranged in death. Perhaps I seem whimsical?"

"You do love children, don't you, Mr. Joyboy?"

"Yes, Miss Thanatogenos. I try not to discriminate, but I am only human. There is something in the innocent appeal of a child that brings out a little more than the best in me. It's as if I was inspired, sometimes, from outside; something higher . . . but I mustn't start on my pet subject now. To work—"

Presently the outfitters came and dressed Sir Francis Hinsley in his shroud, deftly fitting it. Then they lifted him—he was getting rigid—and placed him in the casket.

Aimée went to the curtain which separated the embalming rooms from the cosmetic rooms and attracted the notice of an orderly.

"Will you tell Mr. Joyboy that my Loved One is ready for posing? I think he should come now. He is firming."

Mr. Joyboy turned off a tap and came to Sir Francis Hinsley. He raised the arms and set the hands together, not in a form of prayer, but folded one on the other in resignation. He raised the head, adjusted the pillow and twisted the neck so that a three-quarter face was exposed to view. He stood back, studied his work and then leaned forward again to give the chin a little tilt.

"Perfect," he said. "There are a few places where he's got a little rubbed putting him in the casket. Just go over them once with the brush quite lightly."

"Yes, Mr. Joyboy."

Mr. Joyboy lingered a moment, then turned away.

"Back to baby," he said.

FIVE

HE FUNERAL WAS FIXED FOR THURSDAY; WEDNESDAY
afternoon was the time for leave-taking in the
Slumber Room. That morning Dennis called at
Whispering Glades to see that everything was in order.

He was shown straight to the Orchid Room. Flowers had
arrived in great quantities, mainly from the shop below,
mostly in their "natural beauty." (After consultation the
Cricket Club's fine trophy in the shape of cross bats and
wickets had been admitted. Dr. Kenworthy had himself
given judgement; the trophy was essentially a reminder of
life not of death; that was the crux.) The ante-room was so
full of flowers that there seemed no other furniture or deco-
ration; double doors led to the Slumber Room proper.

Dennis hesitated with his fingers on the handle and was
aware of communication with another hand beyond the pan-
els. Thus in a hundred novels had lovers stood. The door
opened and Aimée Thanatogenos stood quite close to him;
behind her more, many more flowers and all about her a rich
hot-house scent and the low voices of a choir discoursing sacred music from the cornice. At the moment of their meeting
a treble voice broke out with poignant sweetness: "Oh for the
Wings of a Dove."

No breath stirred the enchanted stillness of the two

rooms. The leaded casements were screwed tight. The air came, like the boy's voice, from far away, sterilized and transmuted. The temperature was slightly cooler than is usual in American dwellings. The rooms seemed isolated and unnaturally quiet, like a railway coach that has stopped in the night far from any station.

"Come in, Mr. Barlow."

Aimée stood aside and now Dennis saw that the centre of the room was filled with a great cumulus of flowers. Dennis was too young ever to have seen an Edwardian conservatory in full ball rig but he knew the literature of the period and in his imagination had seen such a picture; it was all there, even the gilt chairs disposed in pairs as though for some starched and jewelled courtship.

There was no catafalque. The coffin stood a few inches from the carpet on a base that was hidden in floral enrichments. Half the lid was open. Sir Francis was visible from the waist up. Dennis thought of the wax-work of Marat in his bath.

The shroud had been made to fit admirably. There was a fresh gardenia in the buttonhole and another between the fingers. The hair was snow-white and parted in a straight line from brow to crown revealing the scalp below, colourless and smooth as though the skin had rolled away and the enduring skull already lay exposed.

The complete stillness was more startling than any violent action. The body looked altogether smaller than life-size now that it was, as it were, stripped of the thick pelt of mobility and intelligence. And the face which inclined its blind eyes towards him—the face was entirely horrible; as ageless as a

tortoise and as inhuman; a painted and smirking obscene
travesty by comparison with which the devil-mask Dennis
had found in the noose was a festive adornment, a thing an
uncle might don at a Christmas party.

Aimée stood beside her handiwork—the painter at the
private view—and heard Dennis draw his breath in sudden
emotion.

"Is it what you hoped?" she asked.

"More"—and then—"Is he quite hard?"

"Firm."

"May I touch him?"

"Please not. It leaves a mark."

"Very well."

Then in accordance with the etiquette of the place, she left
him to his reflections.

There was brisk coming-and-going in the Orchid Slumber
Room later that day; a girl from the Whispering Glades secretariat sat in the ante-room recording the names of the visitors. These were not the most illustrious. The stars, the
producers, the heads of departments would come next day
for the interment. That afternoon they were represented by
underlings. It was like the party held on the eve of a wedding
to view the presents, attended only by the intimate, the idle
and the unimportant. The Yes-men were there in force. Man
proposed. God disposed. These bland, plump gentlemen sig-
nalled their final, abiding assent to the arrangement, nodding
into the blind mask of death.

Sir Ambrose made a cursory visit.

"Everything set for tomorrow, Barlow? Don't forget your ode. I should like it at least an hour before the time so that I can run over it in front of the mirror. How is it going?"

"I think it will be all right."

"I shall recite it at the graveside. In the church there will be merely the reading from the Works and a song by Juanita—'The Wearing of the Green.' It's the only Irish song she's learned yet. Curious how flamenco she makes it sound. Have you arranged the seating in the church?"

"Not yet."

"The Cricket Club will be together of course. Megalopolitan will want the first four rows. Erikson is probably coming himself. Well, I can leave all that to you, can't I?" As he left the mortuary he said: "I am sorry for young Barlow. He must feel all this terribly. The great thing is to give him plenty to do."

Dennis presently drove to the University Church. It was a small, stone building whose square tower rose among immature holm-oaks on the summit of a knoll. The porch was equipped with an apparatus by which at will a lecture might be switched on to explain the peculiarities of the place. Dennis paused to listen.

The voice was a familiar one, that of the travel-film: "You are standing in the Church of St. Peter-without-the-walls, Oxford, one of England's oldest and most venerable places of worship. Here generations of students have come from all over the world to dream the dreams of youth. Here scientists and statesmen still unknown dreamed of their future triumphs. Here Shelley planned his great career in poetry. From here young men set out hopefully on the paths of success and happiness. It is a symbol of the soul of the Loved One who starts from here on the greatest success story of all time. The success that waits for all of us whatever the disappointments of our earthly lives.

"This is more than a replica, it is a reconstruction. A building-again of what those old craftsmen sought to do with their rude implements of by-gone ages. Time has worked its mischief on the beautiful original. Here you see it as the first builders dreamed of it long ago.

"You will observe that the side aisles are constructed solely of glass and grade A steel. There is a beautiful anecdote connected with this beautiful feature. In 1935 Dr. Kenworthy was in Europe seeking in that treasure house of Art something worthy of Whispering Glades. His tour led him to Oxford and the famous Norman church of St. Peter. He found it dark. He found it full of conventional and depressing memorials. 'Why,' asked Dr. Kenworthy, 'do you call it St. Peter-without-the-walls?' and they told him it was because in the old days the city wall had stood between it and the business centre. '*My* church,' said Dr. Kenworthy, 'shall have no walls.' And so you see it today full of God's sunshine and fresh air, birdsong and flowers . . ."

Dennis listened intently to the tones so often parodied yet never rendered more absurd or more hypnotic than the original. His interest was no longer purely technical nor purely satiric. Whispering Glades held him in thrall. In a zone of insecurity in the mind where none but the artist dare trespass, the tribes were mustering. Dennis, the frontier-man, could read the signs.

The voice ceased and after a pause began again: "You are standing in the Church of St. Peter-without-the-walls . . ." Dennis switched off the apparatus, re-entered the settled area and set about his prosaic task.

The secretariat had provided him with type-written name-cards. It was a simple matter to deal them out on the benches. Under the organ was a private pew, separated from the nave by an iron grill and a gauze curtain. Here, when there was a need of it, the bereaved families sat in purdah, hidden from curious glances. This space Dennis devoted to the local gossip-writers.

In half an hour his work was done and he stepped out into the gardens which were no brighter or more flowery or fuller of birdsong than the Norman church.

The unwritten verses lay heavy on him. Not a word was yet written and the languorous, odorous afternoon did not conduce to work. There was also another voice speaking faintly and persistently, calling him to a more strenuous task than Frank Hinsley's obsequies. He left his car at the lychgate and followed a gravel walk which led downhill. The graves were barely visible, marked only by little bronze plaques, many of them as green as the surrounding turf. Water played everywhere from a buried network of pipes, making a glittering rain-belt waist-high, out of which rose a host of bronze and Carrara statuary, allegorical, infantile or erotic. Here a bearded magician sought the future in the obscure depths of what seemed to be a plaster football. There a toddler clutched to its stony bosom a marble Mickey Mouse. A turn in the path disclosed Andromeda, naked and fettered in ribbons, gazing down her polished arm at a marble butterfly which had settled there. And all the while his literary sense was alert, like a hunting hound. There was something in Whispering Glades that was necessary to him, that only he could find.

At length he found himself on the margin of a lake, full of lilies and water-fowl. A notice said: "Tickets here for the Lake Island of Innisfree" and three couples of young people stood at the foot of a rustic landing stage. He took a ticket.

"Just the one?" asked the lady at the *guichet*.

The young people were as abstracted as he, each pair lapped in an almost visible miasma of adolescent love. Dennis stood unregarded until at length an electric launch drew out of the opposing shore and came silently to its mooring. They embarked together and after a brief passage the couples slipped away into the gardens. Dennis stood irresolutely on the bank.

The coxswain said: "Expecting someone to meet you here, kid?"

"No."

"There've been no single dames all afternoon. I'd have noticed if there had been. Mostly folk comes in couples. Once in a while a guy has a date here and then more often than not the dame never shows up. Better get the dame before you get the ticket I guess."

"No," said Dennis. "I have merely come to write a poem. Would this be a good place?"

"I wouldn't know, kid. I never wrote a poem. But they've certainly got it fixed up poetic. It's named after a very fancy

poem. They got bee-hives. Once they had bees, too, but folks
was always getting stung so now it's done mechanical and
scientific; no sore fannies and plenty of poetry.

"It certainly is a poetic place to be planted in. Costs round
about a thousand bucks. The poeticest place in the whole
darn park. I was here when they made it. They figured the
Irish would come but it seems the Irish are just naturally poetic and won't pay that much for plantings. Besides, they've
got a cemetery of their own down town, being Catholic. It's
mostly the good-style Jews we get here. They appreciate the
privacy. It's the water you see keeps out the animals. Animals
are a headache in cemeteries. Dr. Kenworthy made a crack
about that one Annual. Most cemeteries, he says, provide a
dog's toilet and a cat's motel. Pretty smart, huh? Dr. Kenworthy is a regular guy when it comes to the Annual.

"No trouble with dogs and cats on the island. Dames is
our headache, dames and guys in very considerable numbers
come here to neck. I reckon they appreciate the privacy, too,
same as cats."

While he spoke some young people had emerged from the
bosky and stood waiting his summons to embark; Paolos and
Francescas emerging from their nether world in an incandes-
cent envelope of oblivious love. One girl blew bubbles of
gum like a rutting camel but her eyes were wide and soft with
remembered pleasure.

In contrast to the ample sweep of surrounding parkland,
the Lake Island was cosy. An almost continuous fringe of
shrub screened its shores from observation. Paths of mown
grass wandered between leafy clumps, opened out into en-

closed funerary glades, and converged on a central space,
where stood a wattle cabin, nine rows of haricots (which by
a system of judicious transplantation were kept in perpet-
ual scarlet flower) and some wicker hives. Here the sound
of bees was like a dynamo, but elsewhere in the island it
came as a gentle murmur hardly distinguishable from the
genuine article.

The graves nearest to the apiary were the most costly of
all but no more conspicuous than those elsewhere in the park;
simple bronze plaques, flush with the turf, bore the most august names in the commercial life of Los Angeles. Dennis
looked into the hut and withdrew apologizing to the disturbed occupants. He looked into the hives and saw in the
depths of each a tiny red eye which told that the sound-
apparatus was working in good order.

It was a warm afternoon; no breeze stirred the evergreens;
peace came dropping slow, too slow for Dennis.

He followed a divergent path and presently came to a little green cul-de-sac, the family burial plot, a plaque in-
formed him, of a great fruiterer. Kaiser's Stoneless Peaches
raised their rosy flock cheeks from every greengrocer's window in the land. Kaiser's Radio Half-hour brought Wagner
into every kitchen. Here already lay two Kaisers, wife and
aunt. Here in the fulness of time would lie Kaiser himself. A
gunnera spread a wide lowly shelter over the place. Dennis
lay down in its dense shade. The apiary, at this distance,
came near to verisimilitude. Peace came dropping rather
more quickly.

He had brought pencil and note book with him. It was not

thus that he wrote the poems which brought him fame and his present peculiar fortune. They had taken their shapes in frigid war-time railway journeys—the racks piled high with equipment, the dimmed lights falling on a dozen laps, the faces above invisible, cigarette-smoke mixing with frosty breath; the unexplained stops, the stations dark as the empty footways. He had written them in Nissen huts and in spring evenings, on a bare heath, a mile from the airfield, and on the metal benches of transport planes. It was not thus that one day he would write what had to be written: not here that the spirit would be appeased which now more faintly pressed its mysterious claim. This high hot afternoon was given for reminiscence rather than for composition. Rhythms from the anthologies moved softly through his mind.

He wrote:

> *Bury the great Knight*
> *With the studio's valediction*
> *Let us bury the great Knight*
> *Who was once the arbiter of popular fiction.*

And:

> *They told me, Francis Hinsley, they told me you were hung*
> *With red protruding eye-balls and black protruding tongue*
> *I wept as I remembered how often you and I*
> *Had laughed about Los Angeles and now 'tis here you'll lie;*
> *Here pickled in formaldehyde and painted like a whore,*
> *Shrimp-pink incorruptible, not lost nor gone before.*

He gazed up into the rhubarb roof. A peach without a
stone. That was the metaphor for Frank Hinsley. Dennis re-
called that he had once tried to eat one of Mr. Kaiser's much-
advertised products and had discovered a ball of damp, sweet
cotton-wool. Poor Frank Hinsley, it was very like him.

This was no time for writing. The voice of inspiration
was silent; the voice of duty muffled. The night would
come when all men could work. Now was the time to watch
the flamingoes and meditate on the life of Mr. Kaiser. Dennis turned on his face and studied the counterfeit handwrit-
ing of the women of the house. Not forceful characters it
seemed. Kaiser owed nothing to women. The stoneless
peach was his alone.

Presently he heard steps approach and, without moving,
could see that they were a woman's. Feet, ankles, calves came
progressively into view. Like every pair in the country they
were slim and neatly covered. Which came first in this
strange civilization, he wondered, the foot or the shoe, the
leg or the nylon stocking? Or were these uniform elegant
limbs, from the stocking-top down, marketed in one cello-
phane envelope at the neighbourhood-store? Did they clip
by some labour-saving device to the sterilized rubber priva-
cies above? Did they come from the same department as the
light irrefragable plastic head? Did the entire article come off
the assembly-lines ready for immediate home-service?

Dennis lay quite still and the girl came within a yard, knelt
down in the same shade and prepared to recline beside him
before she said, "Oh."

Dennis sat up and turning saw the girl from the mortuary.

She was wearing very large, elliptical violet sun-glasses which she now removed to stare the closer and recognize him.

"Oh," she said, "pardon me. Aren't you the friend of the strangulated Loved One in the Orchid Room? My memory's very bad for live faces. You did startle me. I didn't expect to find anyone here."

"Have I taken your place?"

"Not really. I mean it's Mr. Kaiser's place, not mine or yours. But it's usually deserted at this time so I've taken to coming here after work and I suppose I began to think of it as mine. I'll go some other place."

"Certainly not. I'll go. I only came here to write a poem."

"A *poem*."

He had said something. Until then she had treated him with that impersonal insensitive friendliness which takes the place of ceremony in that land of waifs and strays. Now her eyes widened. "Did you say a *poem?*"

"Yes. I am a poet, you see."

"Why, but I think that's wonderful. I've never seen a live poet before. Did you know Sophie Dalmeyer Krump?"

"No."

"She's in Poets' Corner now. She came during my first month when I was only a novice-cosmetician, so of course I wasn't allowed to work on her. Besides she passed on in a street car accident and needed special treatment. But I took the chance to study her. She had very marked Soul. You might say I learned Soul from studying Sophie Dalmeyer Krump. Now whenever we have a treatment needing special Soul, Mr. Joyboy gives it to me."

THE LOVED ONE

"Would you have me, if I passed on?"

"You'd be difficult," she said, examining him with a professional eye. "You're the wrong age for Soul. It seems to come more naturally in the very young or the very old. But I'll certainly do my best. I think it's a very, very wonderful thing to be a poet."

"But you have a very poetic occupation here."

He spoke lightly, teasing, but she answered with great gravity. "Yes, I know. I know I have really. Only sometimes at the end of a day when I'm tired I feel as if it was all rather ephemeral. I mean you and Sophie Dalmeyer Krump write a poem and it's printed and maybe read on the radio and millions of people hear it and maybe they'll still be reading it in hundreds of years' time. While my work is burned sometimes within a few hours. At the best it's put in the mausoleum and even there it deteriorates, you know. I've seen painting there not ten years old that's completely lost tonality. Do you think anything can be a great art which is so impermanent?"

"You should regard it as being like acting or singing or playing an instrument."

"Yes, I do. But nowadays they can make a permanent record of them, too, can't they?"

"Is that what you brood about when you come here alone?"

"Only lately. At first I used just to lie and think how lucky I was to be here."

"Don't you think that any more?"

"Yes, of course I do really. Every morning and all day while I am at work. It's just in the evenings that something comes over me. A lot of artists are like that. I expect poets are, too, sometimes, aren't they?"

"I wish you'd tell me about your work," said Dennis.

"But you've seen it yesterday."

"I mean about yourself and your work. What made you take it up? Where did you learn? Were you interested in that sort of thing as a child? I'd really be awfully interested to know."

"I've always been Artistic," she said. "I took Art at College as my second subject one semester. I'd have taken it as first subject only Dad lost his money in religion so I had to learn a trade."

"He lost his money in religion?"

"Yes, the Four Square Gospel. That's why I'm called Aimée, after Aimée McPherson. Dad wanted to change the name after he lost his money. I wanted to change it too but it rather stuck. Mother always kept forgetting what we'd changed it to and then she'd find a new one. Once you start changing a name, you see, there's no reason ever to stop. One always hears one that sounds better. Besides you see poor Mother was an alcoholic. But we always came back to Aimée between fancy names and in the end it was Aimée won through."

"And what else did you take at College?"

"Just Psychology and Chinese. I didn't get on so well with Chinese. But, of course, they were secondary subjects, too; for Cultural background."

"Yes. And what was your main subject?"

"Beauticraft."

"Oh."

"You know—permanents, facials, wax—everything you get in a Beauty Parlour. Only, of course, we went in for history and theory too. I wrote my thesis on 'Hairstyling in the Orient.' That was why I took Chinese. I thought it would help, but it didn't. But I got my diploma with special mention for Psychology and Art."

"And all this time between psychology and art and Chinese, you had the mortuary in view?"

"Not at all. Do you really want to hear? I'll tell you because it's really rather a poetic story. You see I graduated in '43 and lots of the girls of my class went to war work but I was never at all interested in that. It's not that I'm unpatriotic. Wars simply don't interest me. Everyone's like that now. Well, I was like that in '43. So I went to the Beverly-Waldorf and worked in the Beauty Parlour, but you couldn't really get away from the war even there. The ladies didn't seem to have a mind for anything higher than pattern bombing. There was one lady who was worse than any of them, called Mrs. Komstock. She came every Saturday morning for a blue rinse and set, and I seemed to take her fancy; she always asked for me; no one else would do, but she never tipped me more than a quarter. Mrs. Komstock had one son in Washington and one in Delhi, a grand-daughter in Italy and a nephew who was high in indoctrination and I had to hear everything about them all until it got so I dreaded Saturday mornings more than any day in the week. Then after a time Mrs. Komstock took sick but that wasn't the end of her. She used to send for me to come up to her apartment every week and she still only gave me a quarter and she still talked about the war just as much only not so sensibly. Then imagine my surprise when one day Mr. Jebb, who was the manager, called me over and said: 'Miss Thanatogenos, here's a thing I hardly like to ask you. I don't know exactly how you'll feel about it, but it's Mrs. Komstock who's dead and her son from Washington is here and he's very anxious to have you fix Mrs. Komstock's hair just as it used to be. It seems there aren't any recent photographs and no one at Whispering Glades knows the style and Colonel Komstock can't exactly describe it. So, Miss Thanatogenos, I was wondering, would you mind very much to oblige Colonel Komstock going over to Whispering Glades and fix Mrs. Komstock like Colonel Komstock remembers?'

"Well, I didn't know quite what to think. I'd never seen a dead person before because Dad left Mother before he died, if he is dead, and Mother went East to look for him when I left College and died there. And I had never been inside Whispering Glades as after we lost our money Mother took to New Thought and wouldn't have it that there was such a thing as death. So I felt quite nervous coming here the first time. And then everything was so different from what I expected. Well you've seen it and you know. Colonel Komstock shook hands and said: 'Young lady, you are doing a truly fine and beautiful action' and gave me fifty dollars.

"Then they took me to the embalming rooms and there was Mrs. Komstock lying on the table in her wedding dress. I shall never forget the sight of her. She was transfigured. That's the only word for it. Since then I've had the pleasure of

showing their Loved Ones to more people than I can count
and more than half of them say: 'Why, they're quite transfigured.' Of course there was no colour in her yet and her hair
was kinda wispy; she was pure white like wax, and so cool and
silent. I hardly dared touch her at first. Then I gave her a
shampoo and her blue rinse and a set just as she always had it,
curly all over and kinda fluffed up where it was thin. Then
while she was drying the cosmetician put the colour on. She
let me watch and I got talking with her and she told me how
there was a vacancy for a novice-cosmetician right at the moment so I went straight back and gave Mr. Jebb my notice.
That was nearly two years ago and I've been here ever since."

"And you don't regret it?"

"Ah, never, never for a moment. What I said just now
about being ephemeral every artist thinks sometimes of his
work, doesn't he? Don't you yourself?"

"And they pay you more than in the Beauty Parlour,
I hope?"

"Yes, a little. But then you see Loved Ones can't tip so that
it works out nearly the same. But it isn't for the money I
work. I'd gladly come for nothing only one has to eat and the
Dreamer insists on our being turned out nicely. It's only in
the last year that I've come really to love the work. Before
that I was just glad to serve people that couldn't talk. Then I
began to realize what a work of consolation it was. It's a
wonderful thing to start every day knowing that you are
going to bring back joy into one aching heart. Of course
mine is only a tiny part of it. I'm just a handmaid to the morticians but I have the satisfaction of showing the final result

and seeing the reaction. I saw it with you, yesterday. You're British and sort of inexpressive but I knew just what you were feeling."

"Sir Francis was transfigured certainly."

"It was when Mr. Joyboy came he sort of made me realize what an institution Whispering Glades really is. Mr. Joyboy's kinda holy. From the day he came the whole tone of the mortuary became greatly elevated. I shall never forget how one morning Mr. Joyboy said to one of the younger morticians: 'Mr. Parks, I must ask you to remember you are not at the Happier Hunting Ground.' "

Dennis betrayed no recognition of that name but he felt a hypodermic stab of thankfulness that he had kept silence when, earlier in their acquaintance, he had considered forming a bond between them by lightly mentioning his trade. It would not have gone down. He merely looked blank and Aimée said: "I don't suppose you'd ever have heard of that. It's a dreadful place here where they bury animals."

"*Not* poetic?"

"I was never there myself but I've heard about it. They try and do everything the same as us. It seems kinda blasphemous."

"And what do you think about when you come here alone in the evenings?"

"Just Death and Art," said Aimée Thanatogenos simply.

"Half in love with easeful death."

"What was that you said?"

"I was quoting a poem.

". . . For many a time
I have been half in love with easeful death.
Call'd him soft names in many a mused rhyme,
To take into the air my quiet breath;
Now more than ever seems it rich to die,
To cease upon the midnight with no pain . . ."

"Did you write that?"

Dennis hesitated. "You like it?"

"Why it's beautiful. It's just what I've thought so often and haven't been able to express. 'To make it rich to die' and 'to cease upon the midnight *with no pain.*' That's exactly what Whispering Glades exists for, isn't it. I think it's wonderful to be able to write like that. Did you write it after you came here first?"

"It was written long before."

"Well it couldn't be more lovely if you'd written it in Whispering Glades—on the Lake Island itself. Was it something like that you were writing when I came along?"

"Not exactly."

Across the water the carillon in the Belfry Beautiful musically announced the hour.

"That's six o'clock. I have to go early today."

"And I have a poem to finish."

"Will you stay and do it here?"

"No. At home. I'll come with you."

"I'd love to see the poem when it's done."

"I'll send it to you."

"Aimée Thanatogenos is my name. I live quite close but send it here, to Whispering Glades. This is my true home."

When they reached the ferry the water-man looked at Dennis with complicity. "So she turned up all right, kid," he said.

SIX

M R. JOYBOY WAS DEBONNAIRE IN ALL HIS PROFES-
sional actions. He peeled off his rubber gloves like
a hero of Ouida returning from stables, tossed
them into a kidney bowl and assumed the clean pair which his
assistant held ready for him. Next he took a visiting card—
one of a box of blanks supplied to the florist below—and a
pair of surgical scissors. In one continuous movement he cut
an ellipse, then snicked half an inch at either end along the
greater axis. He bent over the corpse, tested the jaw and
found it firm set; he drew back the lips and laid his card along
the teeth and gums. Now was the moment; his assistant
watched with never-failing admiration the deft flick of the
thumbs with which he turned the upper corners of the card,
the caress of the rubber finger-tips with which he drew the
dry and colourless lips into place. And, behold, where before
had been a grim line of endurance, there was now a smile! It
was masterly. It needed no other touch. Mr. Joyboy stood
back from his work, removed the gloves and said: "For Miss
Thanatogenos."

Of recent weeks the expressions that greeted Aimée from
the trolley had waxed from serenity to jubilance. Other girls
had to work on faces that were stern or resigned or plumb vacant; there was always a nice bright smile for Aimée.

These attentions were noted sourly in the cosmetic rooms where love of Mr. Joyboy illumined the working hours of all the staff. In the evenings each had her consort or suitor; none seriously aspired to be Mr. Joyboy's mate. As he passed among them, like an art-master among his students, with a word of correction here or commendation there, sometimes laying his gentle hand on a living shoulder or a dead haunch, he was a figure of romance, a cult shared by all in common, not a prize to be appropriated by any one of them.

Nor was Aimée entirely at ease in her unique position. That morning in particular she met the corpse's greeting with impaired frankness for she had taken a step which she knew Mr. Joyboy could not possibly approve.

There was a spiritual director, an oracle, in these parts who daily filled a famous column in one of the local newspapers. Once, in days of family piety, it bore the title "Aunt Lydia's Post Bag"; now it was "The Wisdom of the Guru Brahmin," adorned with the photograph of a bearded and almost naked sage. To this exotic source resorted all who were in doubt or distress.

It might be thought that at this extremity of the New World unceremonious manners and frank speech occasioned no doubt; the universal good humour no distress. But it was not so—etiquette, child-psychology, aesthetics and sex reared their questioning heads in this Eden too, and to all readers the Guru Brahmin offered solace and solution.

To him Aimée had applied some time ago when the smiles had first become unequivocal. Her problem was not about Mr. Joyboy's intentions but about her own. The answer had not been quite satisfactory: *"No, A. T., I do not consider that you are in love—yet.* *Esteem for a man's character and admiration of his business ability may form the basis of an improving friendship but they are not Love. What you describe of your feelings in his presence does not incline us to believe that there is a physical affinity between you—yet. But remember love comes late to many. We know cases who have only experienced real love after several years of marriage and the arrival of Junior. See plenty of your friend. Love may come."*

That had been before Dennis Barlow brought a further perplexity to her conscience. It was now six weeks since she met him on the Lake Island, and that morning on the way to work she had posted a letter which had occupied half her night in writing. It was indeed the longest letter she had ever written:

> Dear Guru Brahmin,
> You may remember that I wrote to you in May last for your advice. This time I am enclosing a stamped and addressed envelope for a private answer as I am going to say things I should not like to have referred to in print. Please reply by return or anyway as soon as convenient as I am very worried and must soon do something about it.
> In case you do not remember I will remind you that I work in the same business with a man who is head of the department and in every way the most wonderful character I

can imagine. It is a great privilege to be
associated with one who is so successful
and defined, a natural leader, artist and
model of breeding. In all sorts of little
ways he has made it plain that he prefers
me to the other girls and though he has not
said so yet because he is not the sort to do
so lightly I am sure he loves me
honourably. But I do not have the same
feelings when I am with him as the girls say
they have when they are with their boys
and what one sees in the movies.

But I think I do have such feelings about
another but he is not at all such an admirable
character. First he is British and therefore in
many ways quite Un-American. I do not mean
just his accent and the way he eats but he is
cynical at things which should be Sacred. I do
not think he has any religion. Neither have I
because I was progressive at College and had
an unhappy upbringing as far as religion went
and other things too, but I am ethical. (As this
is confidential I may as well say my mother
was alcoholic which perhaps makes me more
sensitive and reserved than other girls.) He
also has no idea of Citizenship or Social
Conscience. He is a poet and has had a book
printed in England and very well criticized by
the critics there. I have seen the book and

some of the criticisms so I know this is true
but he is very mysterious about what he is
doing here. Sometimes he talks as if he was in
the movies and sometimes as though he did
nothing at all except write poetry. I have seen
his house. He lives alone as the friend (male)
he lived with passed on six weeks ago. I do not
think he goes out with any other girl or is
married. He has not very much money. He is
very distinguished looking in an Un-American
way and very amusing when he is not being
irreverent. Take the Works of Art in
Whispering Glades Memorial Park, he is
often quite irreverent about them which I
think an epitome of all that is finest in the
American Way of Life. So what hope is there
of true happiness?

Also he is not at all cultured. At first I
thought he must be being a poet and he has
been to Europe and seen the Art there but
many of our greatest authors seem to mean
nothing to him.

Sometimes he is very sweet and loving and
then he suddenly becomes unethical and makes
me feel unethical too. So I should value your
advice very highly. Hoping that this long letter
has not been too much,

Cordially yours,
Aimée Thanatogenos.

> He has written a lot of poems to me some of
> them very beautiful and quite ethical others not so
> much.

The knowledge that this letter was in the mail burdened Aimée's conscience and she was grateful when the morning passed without any other sign from Mr. Joyboy than the usual smile of welcome on the trolley. She painted away diligently while at the Happier Hunting Ground Dennis Barlow was also busy.

They had both ovens going and six dogs, a cat and a barbary goat to dispose of. None of the owners was present. He and Mr. Schultz were able to work briskly. The cat and the dogs were twenty-minute jobs. Dennis raked the ashes out while they were still glowing and put them in labelled buckets to cool. The goat took nearly an hour. Dennis looked at it from time to time through the fire-glass pane and finally crushed the horned skull with a poker. Then he turned out the gas, left the oven doors open and prepared the containers. Only one owner had been induced to buy an urn.

"I'm going along now," said Mr. Schultz. "Will you please to wait till they're cold enough to pack up? They're all for home-delivery except the cat. She's for the columbarium."

"Okay, Mr. Schultz. How about the goat's card? We can't very well say he's wagging his tail in heaven. Goats don't wag their tails."

"They do when they go to the can."

"Yes, but it wouldn't look right on the greeting card. They don't purr like cats. They don't sing an orison like birds."

"I suppose they just remember."

Dennis wrote: *Your Billy is remembering you in heaven tonight.*

He stirred the little smoking grey heaps in the bottom of the buckets. Then he returned to the office and resumed his search of the *Oxford Book of English Verse* for a poem for Aimée. He possessed few books and was beginning to run short of material. At first he had tried writing poems for her himself, but she showed a preference for the earlier masters. Moreover, the Muse nagged him. He had abandoned the poem he was writing, long ago it seemed, in the days of Frank Hinsley. That was not what the Muse wanted. There was a very long, complicated and important message she was trying to convey to him. It was about Whispering Glades, but it was not, except quite indirectly, about Aimée. Sooner or later the Muse would have to be placated. She came first. Meanwhile Aimée must draw from the bran-tub of the anthologies. Once he came near to exposure when she remarked that "Shall I compare thee to a summer's day" reminded her of something she had learned at school, and once near to disgrace when she condemned "On thy midnight pallet lying" as unethical. "Now sleeps the crimson petal, now the white," had struck bang in the centre of the bull, but he knew few poems so high and rich and voluptuous. The English poets were proving un-certain guides in the labyrinth of Californian courtship— nearly all were too casual, too despondent, too ceremonious, or too exacting; they scolded, they pleaded, they extolled. Dennis required salesmanship; he sought to present Aimée with an irresistible picture not so much of her own merits or even of his, as of the enormous gratification he was offering.

The films did it; the crooners did it; but not, it seemed, the English poets.

After half an hour he abandoned the search. The first two dogs were ready to be packed. He shook up the goat, which still glowed under its white and grey surface. There would be no poem for Aimée that day. He would take her instead to the Planetarium.

The embalmers had the same meals as the rest of the mortuary staff, but they ate apart at a central table where by recent, but hallowed, tradition they daily spun a wire cage of dice and the loser paid the bill for them all. Mr. Joyboy spun, lost, and cheerfully paid. They always broke about even on the month. The attraction of the gamble was to show that they were men to whom ten or twenty dollars less or more at the end of the week was not a matter of great concern.

At the door of the canteen Mr. Joyboy lingered sucking a digestive lozenge. The girls came out in ones or twos lighting their cigarettes; among them, alone, Aimée who did not smoke. Mr. Joyboy drew her apart into the formal garden. They stood under an allegorical group representing "the Enigma of Existence."

"Miss Thanatogenos," said Mr. Joyboy, "I want to tell you how much I appreciate your work."

"Thank you, Mr. Joyboy."

"I mentioned it yesterday to the Dreamer."

"Oh, thank you, Mr. Joyboy."

"Miss Thanatogenos, for some time the Dreamer has been

looking forward. You know how he looks forward. He is a man of boundless imagination. He considers that the time has come when women should take their proper place in Whispering Glades. They have proved themselves in the lowlier tasks to be worthy of the higher. He believes moreover that there are many people of delicate sensibility who are held back from doing their duty to their Loved Ones by what I can only call prudery, but which Dr. Kenworthy considers a natural reluctance to expose their Loved Ones to anything savouring in the least degree of immodesty. To be brief, Miss Thanatogenos, the Dreamer intends to train a female embalmer and his choice, his very wise choice, has fallen on you."

"Oh, Mr. Joyboy!"

"Say nothing. I know how you feel. May I tell him you accept?"

"Oh, Mr. Joyboy!"

"And now, if I may intrude a personal note, don't you think this calls for a little celebration? Would you do me the honour of taking supper with me this evening?"

"Oh, Mr. Joyboy, I don't know what to say. I did make a sort of date."

"But that was before you heard the news. That puts rather a different complexion on matters, I guess. Besides, Miss Thanatogenos, it was not my intention that we should be alone. I wish you to come to my home. Miss Thanatogenos, I claim as my right the very great privilege and pleasure of presenting the first lady-embalmer of Whispering Glades to my Mom."

It was a day of high emotion. All that afternoon Aimée

was unable to keep her attention on her work. Fortunately, there was little of importance on hand. She helped the girl in the next cubicle to glue a toupé to a more than usually slippery scalp; she hastily brushed over a male baby with flesh tint; but all the time her mind was in the embalmers' room, attentive to the swish and hiss of the taps, to the coming and going of orderlies with covered kidney bowls, to the low demands for suture or ligature. She had never set foot beyond the oilcloth curtains which screened the embalming-rooms; soon she would have the freedom of them all.

At four o'clock the head cosmetician told her to pack up. She arranged her paints and bottles with habitual care, washed her brushes, and went to the cloakroom to change.

She was meeting Dennis on the lake shore. He kept her waiting, and when he came accepted the news that she was going out to supper with annoying composure. "With the Joyboy?" he said. "That ought to be funny." But she was so full of her news that she could not forbear to tell him. "I say," he said, "that *is* something. How much is it worth?"

"I don't know. I didn't go into the question."

"It's bound to be something handsome. Do you suppose it's a hundred a week?"

"Oh, I don't suppose anyone except Mr. Joyboy gets that."

"Well, fifty, anyway. Fifty is pretty good. We could get married on that."

Aimée stopped in her tracks and stared at him. "What did you say?"

"We can get married, don't you see? It can't be less than fifty, can it?"

"And what, pray, makes you think I should marry you?"

"Why, my dear girl, it's only money that has been holding me back. Now you can keep me, there's nothing to stop us."

"An American man would despise himself for living on his wife."

"Yes, but you see I'm European. We have none of these prejudices in the older civilizations. I don't say fifty is much, but I don't mind roughing it a little."

"I think you're entirely contemptible."

"Don't be an ass. I say, you aren't really in a rage, are you?"

Aimée was really in a rage. She left him abruptly and that evening, before she set out for supper, scrawled a hasty note to the Guru Brahmin: *Please don't bother to answer my letter of this morning. I know my own mind now,* and despatched it to the newspaper-office by special delivery.

With a steady hand Aimée fulfilled the prescribed rites of an American girl preparing to meet her lover—dabbed herself under the arms with a preparation designed to seal the sweatglands, gargled another to sweeten the breath, and brushed into her hair some odorous drops from a bottle labelled: "Jungle Venom"— *"From the depth of the fever-ridden swamp,"* the advertisement had stated, *"where juju drums throb for the human sacrifice, Jeannette's latest exclusive creation* Jungle Venom *comes to you with the remorseless stealth of the hunting cannibal."*

Thus fully equipped for a domestic evening, her mind at ease, Aimée waited for Mr. Joyboy's musical "Hallo, there!" from the front door. She was all set to accept her manifest destiny.

But the evening did not turn out quite as she hoped. Its whole style fell greatly below her expectation. She went out rarely, scarcely at all indeed, and perhaps for this reason had exaggerated notions. She knew Mr. Joyboy as a very glorious professional personage, a regular contributor to *The Casket,* an intimate of Dr. Kenworthy's, the sole sun of the mortuary. She had breathlessly traced with her vermilion brush the inimitable curves of his handiwork. She knew of him as a Rotarian and a Knight of Pythias; his clothes and his car were irreproachably new, and she supposed that when he drove sprucely off into his private life he frequented a world altogether loftier than anything in her own experience. But it was not so.

They travelled a long way down Santa Monica Boulevard before finally turning into a building estate. It was not a prepossessing quarter; it seemed to have suffered a reverse. Many of the lots were vacant, but those which were occupied had already lost their first freshness and the timber bungalow at which they finally stopped was in no way more remarkable than its fellows. The truth is that morticians, however eminent, are not paid like film stars. Moreover, Mr. Joyboy was careful. He saved and he paid insurance. He sought to make a good impression in the world. One day he would have a house and children. Meanwhile anything spent inconspicuously, anything spent on Mom, was money down the drain.

"I never seem to get round to doing anything about the garden," Mr. Joyboy said, as though dimly aware of some unexpressed criticism in Aimée's survey. "This is just a little place I got in a hurry to settle Mom in when we came West."

head on one side and blinked. "Sambo," she said. "Won't you speak to me?"

"Why, Mom, you know that bird hasn't spoken in years."

"He speaks plenty when you're away, don't you, my Sambo?"

The bird put its head on the other side, blinked, and suddenly ruffled his few feathers and whistled like a train. "There," said Mrs. Joyboy. "If I hadn't Sambo to love me I might as well be dead."

There was tinned noodle soup, a bowl of salad with tinned crab compounded in it, there was ice-cream and coffee. Aimée helped carry the trays. Aimée and Mr. Joyboy removed the radio and laid the table. Mrs. Joyboy watched them malevolently from her chair. The mothers of great men often disconcert their son's admirers. Mrs. Joyboy had small angry eyes, frizzy hair, pince-nez on a very thick nose, a shapeless body and positively insulting clothes.

"It isn't how we're used to living nor where we're used to living," she said. "We come from the East and if anyone had listened to me that's where we'd be today. We had a coloured girl in Vermont came in regular—fifteen bucks a week and glad of it. You can't find that here. You can't find anything here. Look at that lettuce. There's more things and cheaper things and better things where we come from. Not that we ever had much of anything seeing all I get to keep house on."

"Mom loves a joke," said Mr. Joyboy.

"Joke! Call it a joke to keep house on what I get *and* visitors coming in." Then, fixing Aimée, she added, "And the girls *work* in Vermont."

He opened the front door, stepped back to allow Aimée t
pass, and then yodelled loudly behind her: "Yoohoo, Mom.
Here we come!"

Hectoring male tones filled the little house. Mr. Joyboy
opened a door and ushered Aimée into the source of the nui-
sance, a radio on the central table of a nondescript living-
room. Mrs. Joyboy sat very near it.

"Sit down quietly," she said, "until this is over."

Mr. Joyboy winked at Aimée. "The old lady hates to miss
the political commentaries," he said.

"Quietly," repeated Mrs. Joyboy, fiercely.

They sat silent for ten minutes until the raucous stream of
misinformation gave place to a gentler voice advocating a
brand of toilet paper.

"Turn it off," said Mrs. Joyboy. "Well, he says there'll be
war again this year."

"Mom, this is Aimée Thanatogenos."

"Very well. Supper's in the kitchen. You can get it when
you like."

"Hungry, Aimée?"

"No, yes! I suppose a little."

"Let's go see what surprise the little lady has been cook-
ing up for us."

"Just what you always have," said Mrs. Joyboy; "I ain't
got the time for surprises."

Mrs. Joyboy turned in her chair towards a strangely veiled
object which stood at her other elbow. She drew the fringe of
a shawl, revealed a wire cage, and in it an almost naked parrot. "Sambo," she said winningly, "Sambo." The bird put its

"Aimée works very hard, Mom; I told you."

"Nice work, too. I wouldn't let a daughter of mine do it. Where's your mother?"

"She went East. I think she died."

"Better dead there than alive here. *Think?* That's all children care nowadays."

"Now, Mom, you've no call to say things like that. You know I care . . ."

Later, at last, the time came when Aimée could decently depart; Mr. Joyboy saw her to the gate.

"I'd drive you home," he said, "only I don't like to leave Mom. The street car passes the corner. You'll be all right."

"Oh, I'll be all right," said Aimée.

"Mom just loved you."

"Did she?"

"Why, yes. I always know. When Mom takes a fancy to people she treats them natural same as she treats me."

"She certainly treated me natural."

"I'll say she did. Yes, she treated you natural and no mistake. You certainly made a great impression on Mom."

That evening before she went to bed Aimée wrote yet another letter to the Guru Brahmin.

SEVEN

———— ✦ ————

THE GURU BRAHMIN WAS TWO GLOOMY MEN AND A bright young secretary. One gloomy man wrote the column, the other, a Mr. Slump, dealt with the letters which required private answers. By the time they came to work the secretary had sorted the letters on their respective desks. Mr. Slump, who was a survival from the days of Aunt Lydia and retained her style, usually had the smaller pile, for most of the Guru Brahmin's correspondents liked to have their difficulties exposed to the public. It gave them a sense of greater importance and also, on occasions, led to correspondence with other readers.

The scent of "Jungle Venom" still clung to Aimée's writing paper.

"Dear Aimée," Mr. Slump dictated, adding a link to his endless chain of cigarettes, "I am the tiniest bit worried by the tone of your last letter."

The cigarettes Mr. Slump smoked were prepared by doctors, so the advertisements declared, with the sole purpose of protecting his respiratory system. Yet Mr. Slump suffered and the young secretary suffered with him, hideously. For the first hours of every day he was possessed by a cough which arose from tartarean depths and was relieved only by whisky. On bad mornings it seemed to the suffering secretary that Mr.

Slump would vomit. This was one of the bad mornings. He retched, shivered, and wiped his face with his handkerchief.

"A home-loving, home-making American girl should find nothing to complain of in the treatment you describe. Your friend was doing you the highest honour in his power by inviting you to meet his mother and she would not be a mother in the true sense if she had not wished to see you. A time will come, Aimée, when your son will bring a stranger home. Nor do I think it a reflection on him that he helps his mother in the house. You say he looked undignified in his apron. Surely it is the height of true dignity to help others regardless of convention. The only explanation of your changed attitude is that you do not love him as he has the right to expect, in which case you should tell him so frankly at the first opportunity.

"You are well aware of the defects of the other friend you mention and I am sure I can leave it to your good sense to distinguish between glamour and worth. Poems are very nice things but—in my opinion—a man who will cheerfully take his part in the humble chores of the home is worth ten glib poets."

"Is that too strong?"

"It *is* strong, Mr. Slump."

"Hell, I feel awful this morning. The girl sounds like a prize bitch anyway."

"We're used to that."

"Yes. Well, tone it down a bit. Here's another one from the woman who bites her nails. What did we advise last time?"

"Meditation on the Beautiful."

"Tell her to go on meditating."

Five miles away in the cosmetic room Aimée paused in her work to re-read the poem she had received that morning from Dennis.

God set her brave eyes wide apart, she read,
And painted them with fire;
They stir the ashes of my heart
To embers of desire . . .

Her body is a flower, her hair
About her neck doth play;
I find her colours everywhere,
They are the pride of day.

Her little hands are soft and when
I see her fingers move,
I know in very truth that men
Have died for less than love.
Ah, dear, live lovely thing! My eyes
Have sought her like a prayer . . .

A single tear ran down Aimée's cheek and fell on the smiling waxy mask below her. She put the manuscript into the pocket of her linen smock and her little soft hands began to move over the dead face.

At the Happier Hunting Ground Dennis said: "Mr. Schultz, I want to improve my position."

"It can't be done, not at present. The money just isn't here in the business. You know that as well as I do. You're getting five bucks more than the man before you. I don't say you aren't worth it, Dennis. If business looks up you're the first for a raise."

"I'm thinking of getting married. My girl doesn't know I work here. She's romantic. I don't know she'd think well of this business."

"Have you anything better to go to?"

"No."

"Well, you tell her to lay off being romantic. Forty bucks a week regular is forty bucks."

"Through no wish of my own I have become the protagonist of a Jamesian problem. Do you ever read any Henry James, Mr. Schultz?"

"You know I don't have the time for reading."

"You don't have to read much of him. All his stories are about the same thing—American innocence and European experience."

"Thinks he can outsmart us, does he?"

"James was the innocent American."

"Well, I've no time for guys running down their own folks."

"Oh, he doesn't run them down. The stories are all tragedies one way or another."

"Well, I ain't got the time for tragedies neither. Take an end of this casket. We've only half-an-hour before the pastor arrives."

There was a funeral with full honours that morning, the first for a month. In the presence of a dozen mourners the coffin of an Alsatian was lowered into the flower-lined tomb. The Reverend Errol Bartholomew read the service.

"Dog that is born of bitch hath but a short time to live, and is full of misery. He cometh up, and is cut down like a flower; he fleeth as it were a shadow, and never continueth in one stay . . ."

Later in the office, as he gave Mr. Bartholomew his cheque, Dennis said: "Tell me, how does one become a non-sectarian clergyman?"

"One has the Call."

"Yes, of course; but after the Call, what is the process? I mean is there a non-sectarian bishop who ordains you?"

"Certainly not. Anyone who has received the Call has no need for human intervention."

"You just say one day 'I am a non-sectarian clergyman' and set up shop?"

"There is considerable outlay. You need buildings. But the banks are usually ready to help. Then, of course, what one aims at is a radio congregation."

"A friend of mine has the Call, Mr. Bartholomew."

"Well, I should advise him to think twice about answering it. The competition gets hotter every year, especially in Los Angeles. Some of the recent non-sectarians stop at nothing—not even at psychiatry and table-turning."

"That's bad."

"It is entirely without scriptural authority."

"My friend was thinking of making a speciality of funeral work. He has connections."

"Chicken feed, Mr. Barlow. There is more to be made in weddings and christenings."

"My friend doesn't feel quite the same about weddings and christenings. What he needs is Class. You would say, would you not, that a non-sectarian clergyman was the social equal of an embalmer?"

"I certainly would, Mr. Barlow. There is a very deep respect in the American heart for ministers of religion."

The Wee Kirk o' Auld Lang Syne lies on an extremity of the park out of sight from the University Church and the Mausoleum. It is a lowly building without belfry or ornament, designed to charm rather than to impress, dedicated to Robert Burns and Harry Lauder, souvenirs of whom are exhibited in an annex. The tartan carpet alone gives colour to the interior. The heather which was originally planted round the walls flourished too grossly in the Californian sun, outgrew Dr. Kenworthy's dream so that at length he uprooted it and had the immediate area walled, levelled and paved, giving it the air of a school-yard well in keeping with the high educational traditions of the race it served. But unadorned simplicity and blind fidelity to tradition were alike foreign to the Dreamer's taste. He innovated; two years before Aimée came to Whispering Glades, he introduced into this austere spot a Lovers' Nook; not a lush place comparable to the Lake Isle which invited to poetic dalliance, but something, as it seemed to him, perfectly Scottish; a place where a bargain could be driven and a contract sealed. It consisted of a dais and a double throne of rough-hewn granite. Between the two seats thus formed stood a slab pierced by a heart-shaped aperture. Behind was the inscription:

THE LOVER'S SEAT

THIS SEAT IS MADE OF AUTHENTIC OLD SCOTCH STONE FROM THE HIGHLANDS OF ABERDEEN. IN IT IS INCORPORATED THE ANCIENT SYMBOL OF THE HEART OF THE BRUCE. ACCORDING TO THE TRADITION OF THE GLENS LOVERS WHO PLIGHT THEIR TROTH ON THIS SEAT AND JOIN THEIR LIPS THROUGH THE HEART OF THE BRUCE SHALL HAVE MANY A CANTY DAY WITH ANE ANITHER AND MAUN TOTTER DOWN HAND IN HAND LIKE THE IMMORTAL ANDERSON COUPLE.

The words of the prescribed oath were cut on the step so that a seated couple could conveniently recite them:

TILL A THE SEAS GANG DRY MY DEAR
AND THE ROCKS MELT WI THE SUN;
I WILL LUVE THEE STILL MY DEAR,
WHILE THE SANDS O LIFE SHALL RUN.

The fancy caught the popular taste and the spot is much frequented. Little there tempts the lounger. The ceremony is over in less than a minute, and on most evenings couples may be seen waiting their turn while strange accents struggle with a text which acquires something of the sanctity of mumbo-jumbo on the unpractised lips of Balts and Jews and Slavs. They kiss through the hole and yield place to the next couple, struck silent as often as not with awe at the mystery they have enacted. There is no bird-song here. Instead the skirl of the pipes haunts the pines and the surviving forest-growth of heather.

Here, a few days after her supper with Mr. Joyboy, a newly resolute Aimée led Dennis and, as he surveyed the incised quotations which, in the manner of Whispering Glades, abounded in the spot, he was thankful that a natural abhorrence of dialect had prevented him from borrowing any of the texts of his courtship from Robert Burns.

They waited their turn and presently sat side by side on the double throne. "Till a' the seas gang dry, my dear," whispered Aimée. Her face appeared deliciously at the little window. They kissed, then gravely descended and passed through waiting couples without a glance.

"What is a 'canty day,' Dennis?"

"I've never troubled to ask. Something like hogmanay, I expect."

"What is that?"

"People being sick on the pavement in Glasgow."

"Oh!"

"Do you know how the poem ends? 'Now we maun totter down, John, But hand in hand we'll go, And *sleep together* at the foot, John Anderson my jo.' "

"Dennis, why is all the poetry you know so coarse? And you talking of being a pastor."

"Non-sectarian; but I incline to the Anabaptists in these matters. Anyway, everything is ethical to engaged couples."

After a pause Aimée said: "I shall have to write and tell Mr. Joyboy and the—and someone else."

She wrote that night. Her letters were delivered by the morning post.

Mr. Slump said: "Send her our usual letter of congratulation and advice."

"But, Mr. Slump, she's marrying the wrong one."

"Don't mention that side of it."

Five miles away Aimée uncovered the first corpse of the morning. It came from Mr. Joyboy bearing an expression of such bottomless woe that her heart was wrung.

EIGHT

———————

MR. SLUMP WAS LATE AND CRAPULOUS.
"Another letter from la belle Thanatogenos,"
said Mr. Slump. "I thought we'd had the last of
that dame."

Dear Guru Brahmin,
    Three weeks ago I wrote you that
everything was all right and I had made up my
mind and felt happy but I am still unhappy,
unhappier in a way than I was before.
Sometimes my British friend is sweet to me
and writes poetry but often he wants unethical
things and is so cynical when I say no we must
wait. I begin to doubt we shall ever make a real
American home. He says he is going to be a
pastor. Well as I told you I am progressive and
therefore have no religion but I do not think
religion is a thing to be cynical about because
it makes some people very happy and all
cannot be progressive at this stage of
Evolution. He has not become a pastor yet he
says he has something to do first which he had
promised a man but he doesn't say what it is

and sometimes I wonder is it something wrong
he is so secretive.

Then there is my own career. I was offered a
Big Chance to improve my position and now
no more is said of that. The head of the
department is the gentleman I told you of who
helps his mother in the housework, and since I
plighted my troth with my British friend and
wrote to tell him he never speaks to me even as
much as he speaks professionally to the other
girls of the department. And the place where
we work is meant to be Happy that is one of
the first rules and everyone looks to this
gentleman for an Example and he is very
unhappy, unlike what the place stands for.
Sometimes he even looks mean and that was
the last thing he ever looked before. All my
fiancé does is to make unkind jokes about his
name. I am worried too about the interest he
shows in my work. I mean I think it quite right
a man should show interest in a girl's work but
he shows too much. I mean there are certain
technical matters in any business I suppose
which people do not like to have talked about
outside the office and it is just those matters he
is always asking about . . .

"That's how women always are," said Mr. Slump. "It just
breaks their hearts to let any man go."

*   *   *

There was often a missive waiting for Aimée on her work-table. When they had parted sourly the night before, Dennis transcribed a poem before going to bed and delivered it at the mortuary on his way to work. These missives in his fine script had to fill the place of the missing smiles; the Loved Ones on their trolleys were now as woebegone and re-proachful as the master.

That morning Aimée arrived still sore from the bickering of the preceding evening and found a copy of verses waiting for her. She read them and once more her heart opened to her lover.

> *Aimée, thy beauty is to me*
> *Like those Nicean barks of yore . . .*

Mr. Joyboy passed the cosmetic rooms on his way out, dressed for the street. His face was cast in pitiful gloom. Aimée smiled shyly, deprecating; he nodded heavily and passed by, and then on an impulse she wrote on the top of the lyric: "Try and understand, Aimée," slipped into the embalming room and reverently laid the sheet of paper on the heart of a corpse who was there waiting Mr. Joyboy's attention.

After an hour Mr. Joyboy returned. She heard him enter his room; she heard the taps turned on. It was not until lunch-time that they met.

"That poem," he said, "was a very beautiful thought."

"My fiancé wrote it."

"The Britisher you were with Tuesday?"

"Yes, he's a very prominent poet in England."

"Is that so? I don't ever recall meeting a British poet before. Is that all he does?"

"He's studying to be a pastor."

"Is that so? See here, Aimée, if you have any more of his poems I should greatly appreciate to see them."

"Why, Mr. Joyboy, I didn't know you were one for poems."

"Sorrow and disappointment kinda makes a man poetic I guess."

"I've lots of them. I keep them here."

"I would certainly like to study them. I was at the Knife and Fork Club Dinner last night and I became acquainted with a literary gentleman from Pasadena. I'd like to show them to him. Maybe he'd be able to help your friend some way."

"Why, Mr. Joyboy, that's real chivalrous of you." She paused. They had not spoken so many words to one another since the day of her engagement. The nobility of the man again overwhelmed her. "I hope," she said shyly, "that Mrs. Joyboy is well."

"Mom isn't so good today. She's had a tragedy. You remember Sambo, her parrot?"

"Of course."

"He passed on. He was kinda old, of course, something over a hundred, but the end was sudden. Mrs. Joyboy certainly feels it."

"Oh, I am sorry."

"Yes, she certainly feels it. I've never known her so cast down. I've been arranging for the disposal this morning.

That's why I went out. I had to be at the Happier Hunting
Ground. The funeral's Wednesday. I was wondering, Miss
Thanatogenos: Mom doesn't know so many people in this
State. She certainly would appreciate a friend at the funeral.
He was a sociable bird when he was a bit younger. Enjoyed
parties back East more than anyone. It seems kinda bitter
there shouldn't be anyone at the last rites."

"Why, Mr. Joyboy, of course I'd be glad to come."

"Would you, Miss Thanatogenos? Well, I call that real
nice of you."

Thus at long last Aimée came to the Happier Hunting
Ground.

NINE

A IMÉE THANATOGENOS SPOKE THE TONGUE OF LOS
Angeles; the sparse furniture of her mind—the ob-
jects which barked the intruder's shins—had been
acquired at the local High School and University; she presented herself to the world dressed and scented in obedience
to the advertisements; brain and body were scarcely distinguishable from the standard product, but the spirit—ah, the
spirit was something apart; it had to be sought afar; not here
in the musky orchards of the Hesperides, but in the mountain
air of the dawn, in the eagle-haunted passes of Hellas. An
umbilical cord of cafés and fruit shops, of ancestral shady
businesses (fencing and pimping) united Aimée, all unconscious, to the high places of her race. As she grew up the only
language she knew expressed fewer and fewer of her ripen-
ing needs; the facts which littered her memory grew less substantial; the figure she saw in the looking-glass seemed less
recognizably herself. Aimée withdrew herself into a lofty
and hieratic habitation.

Thus it was that the exposure as a liar and a cheat of the
man she loved, and to whom she was bound by the tenderest
vows, affected only a part of her. Her heart was broken perhaps, but it was a small inexpensive organ of local manufac-
ture. In a wider and grander way she felt that things had been

simplified. She held in her person a valuable concession to bestow; she had been scrupulous in choosing justly between rival claimants. There was no room now for further hesitation. The voluptuous tempting tones of "Jungle Venom" were silenced.

It was, however, in the language of her upbringing that she addressed her final letter to the Guru Brahmin.

Mr. Slump was ill-shaven; Mr. Slump was scarcely sober; "Slump is slipping," said the managing editor. "Have him pull himself up or else fire him." Unconscious of impending doom, Mr. Slump said: "For Christ's sake, Thanatogenos again. What does she say, lovely? I don't seem able to read this morning."

"She has had a terrible awakening, Mr. Slump. The man she thought she loved proves to be a liar and cheat."

"Aw, tell her go marry the other guy."

"That seems to be what she intends doing."

The engagement of Dennis and Aimée had never been announced in any paper and needed no public denial. The engagement of Mr. Joyboy and Aimée had a column-and-a-half in the *Morticians Journal* and a photograph in *The Casket*, while the house-journal *Whispers from the Glades* devoted nearly an entire issue to the romance. A date was fixed for the wedding at the University Church. Mr. Joyboy had been reared a Baptist and the minister who buried the Baptist dead gladly offered his services. The wardrobe-mistress found a white slumber-robe for the bride. Dr. Kenworthy intimated his intention of being there in person. The corpses who came to Aimée for her ministrations now grinned with triumph.

And all this time there was no meeting between Dennis and Aimée. She had last seen him at the parrot's grave when, quite unabashed, it seemed, he had winked at her over the gorgeous little casket. In his heart, however, he had been abashed and thought it well to lie low for a day or two. Then he saw the announcement of the engagement.

It was not an easy matter for Aimée to refuse communication with anyone. She did not live in circumstances where she could say "I am not at home to Mr. Barlow" and order her servants to refuse him admission. She had no servant; if the telephone rang, she answered it. She had to eat. She had to shop. In either case she stood open to those friendly casual-seeming encounters in which American social life abounds. One evening shortly before the wedding-day Dennis lay in wait for her, followed her to a Nutburger counter and took the next stool.

"Hullo, Aimée. I want to talk to you."

"There's nothing you can say means anything now."

"But, my dear girl, you seem to have forgotten that we're engaged to be married. My theological studies are prospering. The day when I shall claim you is at hand."

"I'd rather die."

"Yes, I confess I overlooked that alternative. D'you know, this is the first time I've ever eaten a nutburger? I've often wondered what they were. It is not so much their nastiness as their total absence of taste that shocks one. But let us get this clear. Do you deny that you solemnly swore to marry me?"

"A girl can change her mind, can't she?"

"Well, you know, I don't honestly think she can. You made a very solemn promise."

"Under false pretences. All those poems you sent and pretended you'd written for me, that I thought so cultivated I even learned bits of them by heart—all by other people, some by people who passed on hundreds of years ago. I never felt so mortified as when I found out."

"So that's the trouble, is it? Well, I deny it absolutely."

"You deny sending me poems by people who'd passed on?"

"I deny saying they were by me."

"I'm going now. I don't want to eat anything."

"Well, you chose the place. When I took you out I never gave you nutburgers, did I?"

"As often as not it was *I* took *you* out."

"Well, whoever paid, we always had something better than nutburgers. You can't walk down the street crying like that. I've my car parked across the way. Let me drop you home."

They stepped out into the neon-lighted boulevard. "Now, Aimée," said Dennis, "let us not have a tiff."

"Tiff? I loathe everything about you."

"When we last met we were engaged to be married. I think I am entitled to some explanation. So far, all you have complained of is that I am not the author of some of the best-known poems in the English language. Well, I ask you, is Popjoy?"

"You meant me to think you wrote them."

"There, Aimée, you misjudge me. I am appalled to learn

that you thought anything of the kind. It is I who should be disillusioned when I think that I have been squandering my affections on a girl ignorant of the commonest treasures of literature. But I realize that you have different educational standards from those I am used to. No doubt you know more than I about science and citizenship. But in the dying world I come from quotation is a national vice. No one would think of making an after-dinner speech without the help of poetry. It used to be the classics, now it's lyric verse. Liberal Members of our House of Commons constantly quote Shelley; Tories and Socialists don't get up and complain of being disillusioned when they learn that their ornaments are not original. They keep quiet and pretend they knew all the time."

"I shall never believe anything you say again."

"Well, damn it, what don't you believe?"

"I don't believe in you."

"Ah, that's another point. There's all the difference between believing someone and believing in them."

"Oh, do stop being reasonable."

"Very well." Dennis drew into the side of the road and attempted to take her in his arms. She resisted with fiery agility. He desisted and lit a cigar. Aimée sobbed in the corner and presently said: "That awful funeral."

"The Joyboy parrot? Yes, I think I can explain that. Mr. Joyboy would have an open casket. I advised against it and, after all, I know. I've studied the business. An open casket is all right for dogs and cats who lie down and curl up naturally. But parrots don't. They look absurd with a head on a pillow. But I came up against a blank wall of snobbery. What was done in Whispering Glades must be done at the Happier Hunting Ground. Or do you think that the whole thing was a frame-up? I believe that sanctimonious pest *wanted* the poor parrot to look absurd so as to lower me in your eyes. I believe that's it. Who asked you to the funeral, anyway? Were you acquainted with the late parrot?"

"To think that all the time you were going out with me you were secretly going to *that place* . . ."

"My dear, you as an American should be the last to despise a man from starting at the bottom of the ladder. I can't claim to be as high in the mortuary world as your Mr. Joyboy, but I am younger, very much better looking, and I wear my own teeth. I have a future in the Non-sectarian Church. I expect to be head chaplain at Whispering Glades when Mr. Joyboy is still swilling out corpses. I have the makings of a great preacher—something in the metaphysical seventeenth-century manner, appealing to the intellect rather than to crude emotion. Something Laudian— ceremonious, verbose, ingenious and doctrinally quite free of prejudice. I have been thinking a good deal about my costume, full sleeves, I think . . ."

"Oh, do be quiet! You bore me so."

"Aimée, as your future husband and spiritual director, I must tell you that that is no way to speak of the man you love."

"I don't love you."

" 'Till a' the seas gang dry, my dear.' "

"I haven't the least idea what that means."

" 'And the rocks melt wi' the sun.' That's plain enough, anyway. 'I will luve.' You can't fail to understand those words, surely? It's just the way the crooners pronounce them. 'I will luve thee still my dear, While the sands o' life shall run.' The last words I admit are a little obscure, but the general sense is obvious to the most embittered. Have you forgotten the Heart of the Bruce?"

The sobs ceased, and the ensuing silence told Dennis that intellectual processes were at work in the exquisite dim head in the corner. "Was it Bruce wrote that poem?" she asked at length.

"No; but the names are so similar that the difference is immaterial."

Another pause. "Didn't this Bruce, or whatever he's called, make some way round his oath?"

Dennis had not counted greatly on the ceremony at the Kirk o' Auld Lang Syne. He had introduced it whimsically. Now, however, he pounced on the advantage. "Listen, you delicious, hopeless creature. You are on the horns of a dilemma—which is European for being in a jam."

"Drive me home."

"Very well, I can explain as we go. You think Whispering Glades the most wonderful thing outside heaven. I see your point. In my rough British way I share your enthusiasm. I have been planning an opus on the subject, but I am afraid I can't say with Dowson 'If you ever come to read it, you will understand.' You won't, my dear, not a word of it. All this is by the way. Now, your Mr. Joyboy is the incarnate spirit of Whispering Glades—the one mediating logos between Dr.

Kenworthy and common humanity. Well, we're obsessed by Whispering Glades, both of us—'half in love with easeful death,' as I once told you—and to save further complications let me explain that I did not write that poem either—you're the nautch girl and vestal virgin of the place, and naturally I attach myself to you and you attach yourself to Joyboy. Psychologists will tell you that kind of thing happens every day.

"It may be that by the Dreamer's standards there are defects in my character. The parrot looked terrible in his casket. So what? You loved me and swore to love me eternally with the most sacred oath in the religion of Whispering Glades. So you see the dilemma, jam or *impasse*. Sanctity is indivisible. If it isn't sacred to kiss me through the heart of Burns or Bruce, it isn't sacred to go to bed with old Joyboy."

There was silence still. Dennis had made an impression far beyond his expectation.

"Here you are," he said at length, stopping at Aimée's apartment house. This was not the moment he realized for soft advances. "Jump out."

Aimée said nothing and for a moment did not move. Then in a whisper she said: "You could release me."

"Ah, but I won't!"

"Not when you know I've quite forgotten you?"

"But you haven't."

"Yes. When I turn away I can't even remember what you look like. When you are not there I don't think of you at all."

*　　*　　*

Left to herself in the concrete cell which she called her apartment, Aimée fell victim to all the devils of doubt. She switched on her radio; a mindless storm of Teutonic passion possessed her and drove her to the cliff-edge of frenzy; then abruptly stopped. "This rendition comes to you by courtesy of Kaiser's Stoneless Peaches. Remember, no other peach now marketed is perfect and completely stoneless. When you buy a Kaiser's Stoneless Peach you are buying full weight of succulent peach flesh and nothing else . . ."

She turned to the telephone and dialled Mr. Joyboy's number.

"Please, please come over. I'm so worried."

From the ear-piece came a babel, human and inhuman, and in the midst of it a still small voice saying, "Speak up, honey-baby. I can't quite get you."

"I'm so miserable."

"It isn't just easy hearing you, honey-baby. Mom's got a new bird and she's trying to make him talk. Maybe we better leave whatever it is and talk about it tomorrow."

"Please, dear, come right over now; couldn't you?"

"Why, honey-baby, I couldn't leave Mom the very evening her new bird arrived, could I? How would she feel? It's a big evening for Mom, honey-baby. I have to be here with her."

"It's about our marriage."

"Yes, honey-baby, I kinda guessed it was. Plenty of little problems come up. They all look easier in the morning. Take a good sleep, honey-baby."

"I must see you."

"Now, honey-baby, I'm going to be firm with you. Just

you do what Poppa says this minute or Poppa will be real
mad at you."

She rang off and once more resorted to grand opera; she
was swept up and stupefied in the gust of sound. It was too
much. In the silence that followed her brain came to life a little. Again the telephone. The local newspaper.

"I want to speak to the Guru Brahmin."

"Why, he doesn't work evenings. I'm sorry."

"It's very important. Couldn't you please give me his
home number?"

"There's two of them. Which d'you want?"

"Two? I didn't know. I want the one who answers letters."

"That will be Mr. Slump, but he doesn't work here after
tomorrow, and he wouldn't be home at this time anyway. You
could try Mooney's Saloon. That's where the editorials
mostly go evenings."

"And his real name is Slump?"

"That's what he tells me, sister."

Mr. Slump had that day been discharged from his paper.
Everyone in the office had long expected the event except
Mr. Slump himself, who had taken the story of his betrayal to
several unsympathetic drinking-places.

The barman said: "There's a call for you, Mr. Slump. Are
you here?"

It seemed likely to Mr. Slump in his present state of mind
that this would be his editor, repentant; he reached across the
bar for the instrument.

"Mr. Slump?"

"Yes."

"I've found you at last. I'm Aimée Thanatogenos . . . You remember me?"

It was a memorable name. "Sure," said Mr. Slump at length.

"Mr. Slump, I am in great distress. I need your advice. You remember the Britisher I told you about . . ."

Mr. Slump held the telephone to the ear of the man next to him, grinned, shrugged, finally laid it on the bar, lit a cigarette, took a drink, ordered another. Tiny anxious utterances rose from the stained wood. It took Aimée some time to make her predicament clear. Then the regular flow of sound ceased and gave place to little, spasmodic whispers. Mr. Slump listened again. "Hullo . . . Mr. Slump . . . Are you listening? . . . Did you hear me? . . . hullo!"

"Well, sister, what is it?"

"You heard what I said?"

"Sure, I heard fine."

"Well . . . what am I to do?"

"Do! I'll tell you what to do. Just take the elevator to the top floor. Find a nice window and jump out. That's what you can do." There was a little sobbing gasp and then a quiet "Thank you."

"I told her to go take a high jump."

"We heard."

"Wasn't I right?"

"You know best, brother."

"Well, for Christ's sake, with a name like that!"

In Aimée's bathroom cupboard, among the instruments and chemicals which are the staples of feminine well-being, lay

the brown tube of barbiturates which is the staple of feminine repose. Aimée swallowed her dose, lay down and
awaited sleep. It came at length brusquely, perfunctorily,
without salutation or caress. There was no delicious influx,
touching, shifting, lifting, setting free and afloat the
grounded mind. At 9:40 P.M. she was awake and distraught,
with a painful dry sense of contraction and tension about the
temples; her eyes watered, she yawned; suddenly it was 5:25
A.M. and she was awake once more.

It was still night; the sky was starless and below it the
empty streets flamed with light. Aimée rose and dressed and
went out under the arc lamps. She met no one during the brief
walk from her apartment to Whispering Glades. The Golden
Gates were locked from midnight until morning, but there
was a side door always open for the use of the night-staff.
Aimée entered and followed the familiar road upwards to the
terrace of the Kirk o' Auld Lang Syne. Here she sat and
waited for dawn.

Her mind was quite free from anxiety. Somehow, somewhere in the blank black hours she had found counsel; she
had communed perhaps with the spirits of her ancestors,
the impious and haunted race who had deserted the altars of
the old Gods, had taken ship and wandered, driven by what
pursuing furies through what mean streets and among what
barbarous tongues! Her father had frequented the Four
Square Gospel Temple: her mother drank. Attic voices
prompted Aimée to a higher destiny; voices which far away
and in another age had sung of the Minotaur, stamping far
underground at the end of the passage; which spoke to her

more sweetly of the still Boeotian water-front, the armed men all silent in the windless morning, the fleet motionless at anchor, and Agamemnon turning away his eyes; spoke of Alcestis and proud Antigone.

The East lightened. In all the diurnal revolution these first fresh hours alone are untainted by man. They lie late abed in that region. In exaltation Aimée watched the countless statues glimmer, whiten and take shape while the lawns changed from silver and grey to green. She was touched by warmth. Then suddenly all round her and as far as eye could see the slopes became a dancing surface of light, of millions of minute rainbows and spots of fire; in the control house the man on duty had turned the irrigation cock and water was flooding through the net-work of pierced and buried pipes. At the same time parties of gardeners with barrows and tools emerged and tramped to their various duties. It was full day.

Aimée walked swiftly down the gravelled drive to the mortuary entrance. In the reception-room the night staff were drinking coffee. They glanced at her incuriously as she passed silently through them, for urgent work was done at all hours. She took the lift to the top story where everything was silent and empty save for the sheeted dead. She knew what she wanted and where to find them; a wide-mouthed blue bottle and a hypodermic syringe. She indited no letter of farewell or apology. She was far removed from social custom and human obligations. The protagonists, Dennis and Mr. Joyboy, were quite forgotten. The matter was between herself and the deity she served.

It was quite without design that she chose Mr. Joyboy's work-room for the injection.

TEN

M R. SCHULTZ HAD FOUND A YOUNG MAN TO TAKE Dennis's place and Dennis was spending his last week at the Happier Hunting Ground in showing him the ropes. He was an apt young man much interested in the prices of things.

"He hasn't your personality," said Mr. Schultz. "He won't have the same human touch but I figure he'll earn his keep other ways."

On the morning of Aimée's death Dennis set his pupil to work cleaning the generating-plant of the crematorium and was busy with the correspondence-lessons in preaching to which he now subscribed, when the door of the office opened and he recognized with great surprise his bare acquaintance and rival in love, Mr. Joyboy.

"Mr. Joyboy," he said. "Not another parrot so soon?"

Mr. Joyboy sat down. He looked ghastly. Finding himself alone with Dennis he began to blubber. "It's Aimée," he said.

Dennis answered with high irony: "You have not come to arrange *her* funeral?" upon which Mr. Joyboy cried with sudden passion. "You knew it. I believe you killed her. You killed my honey-baby."

"Joyboy, these are wild words."

"She's dead."

"My fiancée?"

"*My* fiancée."

"Joyboy, this is no time to wrangle. What makes you think she is dead? She was perfectly well at suppertime last night."

"She's there, in my workshop, under a sheet."

"That, certainly, is what your newspapers would call 'factual.' You're sure it's her?"

"Of course I'm sure. She was poisoned."

"Ah! The nutburger?"

"Cyanide. Self-administered."

"This needs thinking about, Joyboy." He paused. "I loved that girl."

"*I* loved her."

"*Please.*"

"She was my honey-baby."

"I must beg you not to intrude these private and rather peculiar terms of endearment into what should be a serious discussion. What have you done?"

"I examined her, then I covered her up. We have some deep refrigerators we sometimes use for half-finished work. I put her in there." He began to weep tempestuously.

"What have you come to me for?"

Mr. Joyboy snorted.

"I can't hear you."

"Help," said Mr. Joyboy. "It's your fault. You've gotta do something."

"This is no time for recrimination, Joyboy. Let me merely point out that you are the man publicly engaged to her. In the circumstances some emotion is natural—but do not go to extremes. Of course I never thought her wholly sane, did you?"

"She was my—"

"Don't say it, Joyboy. Don't say it or I shall turn you out."

Mr. Joyboy fell to more abandoned weeping. The apprentice opened the door and stood momentarily embarrassed at the spectacle.

"Come in," said Dennis. "We have here a client who has just lost a little pet. You will have to accustom yourself to exhibitions of distress in your new rôle. What did you want?"

"Just to say the gas furnace is working fine again."

"Excellent. Well now go and clear the collecting-van. Joyboy," he continued when they were again alone, "I beg you to control yourself and tell me plainly what is in your mind. All I can discern at the moment is a kind of family litany of mommas and poppas and babies."

Mr. Joyboy made other noises.

"That sounded like 'Dr. Kenworthy.' Is that what you are trying to say?"

Mr. Joyboy gulped.

"Dr. Kenworthy knows?"

Mr. Joyboy groaned.

"He does not know?"

Mr. Joyboy gulped.

"You want me to break the news to him?"

Groan.

"You want me to help keep him in ignorance?"

Gulp.

"You know, this is just like table-turning."

"Ruin," said Mr. Joyboy. "Mom."

"You think that your career will suffer if Dr. Kenworthy learns you have the poisoned corpse of our fiancée in the ice-box? For your mother's sake this is to be avoided? You are proposing that I help dispose of the body?"

Gulp, and then a rush of words. "You've gotta help me . . . through you it happened . . . simple American kid . . . phoney poems . . . love . . . Mom . . . baby . . . gotta help . . . gotta . . . gotta."

"I don't like this repetition of 'gotta,' Joyboy. Do you know what Queen Elizabeth said to her Archbishop—an essentially non-sectarian character incidentally? 'Little man, little man, "must" is not a word to be used to princes.' If I help you it will be freely and from the highest motives. Tell me has anyone besides yourself access to this ice-box?" Groan. "Well then go away, Joyboy. Go back to your work. I will give the matter my attention. Come and see me again after luncheon."

Mr. Joyboy went. Dennis heard the car start. Then he went out alone into the pets' cemetery with his own thoughts which were not a thing to be shared with Mr. Joyboy.

Thus musing he was disturbed by a once familiar visitor.

It was a chilly day and Sir Ambrose Abercrombie wore tweeds, cape and deerstalker-cap, the costume in which he had portrayed many travesties of English rural life. He carried a shepherd's crook.

"Ah, Barlow," he said, "still hard at it?"

"One of our easier mornings. I hope it is not a bereavement which brings you here?"

"No, nothing like that. Never kept an animal out here. Miss 'em, I can tell you. Brought up among dogs and horses. Daresay you were, too, so you won't misunderstand me when I say this is no place for them. Wonderful country of course, splendid lot of people, but no one who was really fond of dogs would bring one here." He paused and gazed curiously about him at the modest monuments. "Attractive place you've got here. Sorry to see you're moving."

"You received one of my cards?"

"Yes, got it here. Thought at first it must be someone playing rather a poor kind of joke. It's genuine, is it?"

From the depths of his plaid he produced a printed card and handed it to Dennis. It read:

Squadron Leader the Rev. Dennis Barlow
begs to announce that he is shortly starting business at 1154
Arbuckle Avenue, Los Angeles. All non-sectarian services
expeditiously conducted at competitive prices. Funerals a
speciality. Panegyrics in prose or poetry. Confessions heard
in strict confidence.

"Yes, quite genuine," said Dennis.

"Ah. I was afraid it might be."

Another pause. Dennis said: "The cards were sent out by an agency, you know. I didn't suppose you would be particularly interested."

"But I am particularly interested. Is there somewhere we could go and talk?"

Wondering whether Sir Ambrose was to be his first pen-

itent, Dennis led him indoors. The two Englishmen sat
down in the office. The apprentice popped his head in, to
report well of the collecting-van. At length Sir Ambrose
said: "It won't do, Barlow. You must allow me an old man's
privilege of speaking frankly. It won't do. After all you're
an Englishman. They're a splendid bunch of fellows out
here, but you know how it is. Even among the best you find
a few rotters. You know the international situation as well
as I do. There are always a few politicians and journalists
simply waiting for the chance to take a knock at the Old
Country. A thing like this is playing into their hands. I
didn't like it when you started work here. Told you so
frankly at the time. But at least this is a more or less private
concern. But religion's quite another matter. I expect you're
thinking of some pleasant country rectory at home. Religion's not like that here. Take it from me, I know the place."

"It's odd you should say that, Sir Ambrose. One of my
chief aims was to raise my status."

"Then chuck it, my dear boy, before it's too late." Sir Ambrose spoke at length of the industrial crisis in England, the
need for young men and dollars, the uphill work of the film
community in keeping the flag flying. "Go home, my dear
boy. That is your proper place."

"As a matter of fact," said Dennis, "things have rather
changed with me since that announcement was written. The
Call I heard has grown fainter."

"Capital," said Sir Ambrose.

"But there are certain practical difficulties. I have invested
all my small savings in my theological studies."

"I expected something of the kind. That is where the Cricket Club comes in. I hope the time will never come when we are not ready to help a fellow countryman in difficulties. We had a committee meeting last night and your name was mentioned. There was complete agreement. To put it in a nutshell, my boy, we will send you home."

"First class?"

"Tourist. I'm told it's jolly comfortable. How about it?"

"No drawing-room in the train?"

"No drawing-room."

"Well," said Dennis, "I suppose that as a clergyman I should have had to practise certain austerities."

"Spoken like a man," said Sir Ambrose. "I have the cheque with me. We signed it last night."

Some hours later the mortician returned.

"You have regained command of yourself? Sit down and listen attentively. You have two problems, Joyboy, and let me emphasize that they are *yours*. I am in no way implicated. I resign all rights in the girl. *You* are in possession of the corpse of *your* fiancée and *your* career is threatened. You are a well-known man in your profession and you would never live down the scandal. You have then two problems—to dispose of the body and to explain the disappearance. You have come to me for help and it so happens that in both these things I and only I can help you.

"I have here at my disposal an excellent crematorium. We are happy-go-lucky people at the Happier Hunting Ground. There are no formalities. If I arrive here with a casket and say 'Mr. Schultz, I've a sheep here to incinerate,' he says, 'Go ahead.' Once you seemed inclined to look down on us for our easy manners. Now perhaps you feel differently. All we have to do is to collect our Loved One, if you will forgive the expression, and bring her here. Tonight after working hours will be the time.

"Secondly, to explain the disappearance. Miss Thanatogenos had few acquaintances and no relations. She disappears on the eve of her wedding. It is known that I once favoured her with my attentions. What could be more plausible than that her natural good taste should have triumphed at the last moment and she should have eloped with her earlier lover? All that is necessary is for me to disappear at the same time. No one in Southern California, as you know, ever inquires what goes on beyond the mountains. She and I perhaps may incur momentary condemnation as unethical. You may receive some slightly unwelcome commiseration. There the matter will end.

"For some time I have felt oppressed by the unpoetic air of Los Angeles. I have work to do and this is not the place to do it. It was only our young friend who kept me here—she and penury. And talking of penury, Joyboy, I take it you have substantial savings?"

"I've some insurance."

"What can you borrow on that? Five thousand dollars?"

"No, no, nothing like that."

"Two?"

"No."

"How much then?"

"A thousand maybe."

"Draw it out, Joyboy. We shall need it all. And cash this cheque at the same time. Together it will be enough. It may seem to you sentimental but I wish to leave the United States in the same style as I came. Whispering Glades must not fall below Megalopolitan Studios in hospitality. From your bank go to the travel agency and take me a ticket to England—a drawing-room to New York, Cunarder single state-room with bath from there on. I shall need ready cash for incidental expenses. So bring the rest in a lump sum with the tickets. All understood? Very well. I will be at your mortuary with the collecting-van soon after dinner."

Mr. Joyboy was waiting for Dennis at the side entrance of the mortuary. Whispering Glades was ideally equipped for the smooth movement of bodies. On a swift and silent trolley they set Dennis's largest collecting-box, first empty, later full. They drove to the Happier Hunting Ground where things were more makeshift but between them without great difficulty they man-handled their load to the crematorium, and stowed it in the oven. Dennis turned on the gas and lit it. Flame shot from all sides of the brick oven. He closed the iron door.

"I reckon she'll take an hour and a half," he said. "Do you want to stay?"

"I can't bear to think of her going out like this—she loved to see things done right."

"I rather thought of conducting a service. My first and last non-sectarian office."

"I couldn't bear that," said Mr. Joyboy.

"Very well. I will recite instead a little poem I have written for the occasion.

"Aimée, thy beauty was to me,
　Like those Nicean barks of yore,"

"Hey, you can't say that. That's the phoney poem."
"Joyboy, please remember where you are.

　"That gently, o'er a perfumed sea
　The weary way-worn wanderer bore
　To his own native shore.

"It's really remarkably apposite, is it not?"
But Mr. Joyboy had left the building.

The fire roared in the brick oven. Dennis must wait until all was consumed. Meanwhile he entered the office and made a note in the book kept there for that purpose.

Tomorrow and on every anniversary as long as the Happier Hunting Ground existed a postcard would go to Mr. Joyboy: *Your little Aimée is wagging her tail in heaven tonight, thinking of you.*

"Like those Nicean barks of yore," he repeated:

　"That gently, o'er a perfumed sea,
　The weary way-worn wanderer bore
　To his own native shore."

On this last evening in Los Angeles Dennis knew that he was singularly privileged. The strand was littered with bones and wreckage. He was adding his bit; something that had long irked him, his young heart. He was carrying back instead a great, shapeless chunk of experience, the artist's load; bearing it home to his ancient and comfortless shore; to work on it hard and long, for God knew how long—it was the moment of vision for which a lifetime is often too short.

He picked up the novel which Miss Poski had left on his desk and settled down to await his loved one's final combustion.

ABOUT THE AUTHOR

EVELYN WAUGH (1903–1966) was born in Hampstead, England, into a family of publishers and writers. He was educated at Lancing and at Hertford College, Oxford, where he majored in journalism and modern history.

Waugh's first book, a life of Dante Gabriel Rossetti, was published in 1928. Soon afterward his first novel, *Decline and Fall*, appeared and his career was sensationally launched. "In fifteen novels of cunning construction and lapidary eloquence," *Time* summarized later, "Evelyn Waugh developed a wickedly hilarious yet fundamentally religious assault on a century that, in his opinion, had ripped up the nourishing taproot of tradition and let wither all the dear things of the world." Waugh's celebrated novels include *Vile Bodies*, *A Handful of Dust*, *Scoop*, *Black Mischief*, *Put Out More Flags*, *Brideshead Revisited*, *Sword of Honor* (a trilogy comprising *Men at Arms*, *Officers and Gentlemen*, and *The End of the Battle*), *The Loved One*, and *The Ordeal of Gilbert Pinfold*. He also wrote several acclaimed travel books, two additional biographies, and an autobiography, *A Little Learning*. His short fiction was recently collected in *The Complete Stories of Evelyn Waugh*.